Burton's Zoom Zoom Va-ROOOM Machine

by Dorothy Haas

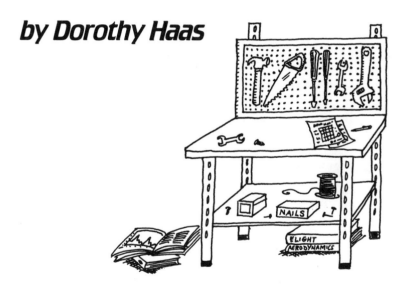

BRADBURY PRESS
New York

Collier Macmillan Canada
Toronto
Maxwell Macmillan International Publishing Group
New York   Oxford   Singapore   Sydney

Bradbury Press
Macmillan Publishing Company
866 Third Avenue
New York, NY 10022

Collier Macmillan Canada, Inc.
1200 Eglinton Avenue East
Suite 200
Don Mills, Ontario M3C 3N1

First edition
Printed in the United States of America
1   2   3   4   5   6   7   8   9   10

Library of Congress Cataloging-in-Publication Data
Haas, Dorothy F.
    Burton's zoom zoom va-rooom machine / by Dorothy Haas.
        p.   cm.
    Summary: Evil Professor Savvy tries to steal Burton's newest
invention, a rocket-powered skateboard.
    ISBN 0-02-738201-X
    [1. Inventors—Fiction.]   I. Title.   PZ7.H1124Bu   1990
[Fic]—dc20   89-77426   CIP   AC

The text of this book is set in Caledonia.
The illustrations are rendered in ink.
Book design by Cathy Bobak

Dedicated to all girls and boys
who like to read
just for the fun of it

Contents

1

Burton's Best Invention

Burton Bell Whitney Knockwurst was an inventor.
He came by it naturally. Inventing ran in his family.
His father invented music—he was a composer. His
mother invented ideas—she worked for a think
tank. His big sister, Edisonia, was an inventor—
she was inventing a new kind of musical instrument.
Burton had a little brother, too. But nobody talked
about him.

Burton was getting on in years. He was eleven
years old. That's pretty elderly for inventing. But

1

Burton had good inventing credits behind him.

When he was four, Burton had taken apart the clock in his bedroom—a bunny in a blue sailor suit. When he put it back together, that bunny twitched its nose every hour on the hour.

When he was six, Burton rigged the orange juice squeezer to the toaster. The heat from the toaster turned the squeezer. Just as the toast was nicely brown, the juice was ready without another drop left in the orange. Nobody had to put a hand on the orange. And the invention saved the Knockwursts a lot on their electric bill, too.

The best thing Burton had ever invented was an automatic dog washer.

There had been a time when the Knockwursts' dachshund, Clinton, would run and hide every time someone said *bath*. Even when they spelled it— b-a-t-h—Clinton hid behind the water heater. And then when he got into the tub, he would close his eyes tight and shiver and shake, spraying water all over everyone. He looked absolutely miserable. What could be done for poor Clinton?

After a whole lot of thinking, Burton decided what was needed was an automatic dog washer. He made one. Clinton went into it willingly because at the far end of it was a really awesome bone. Clinton could see that bone the whole time he was being bathed.

Inside the automatic dog washer were a soaper and brushes and a rinser and a blow drier made from Mama Knockwurst's old hair drier. Air from the drier blew across the bone right at Clinton's nose. That wonderful smell held his interest while the terrible soaping and scrubbing were going on. Clinton learned to put up with it, his eyes on the bone, sniffing happily. When he got into the drier, he positively grinned, eyeing the bone that would soon be his.

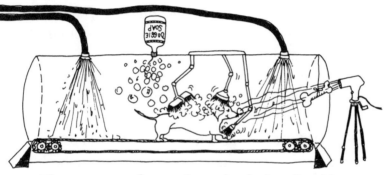

The automatic dog washer solved a lot of problems in the Knockwurst household.

But now Burton was eleven, and it was time to get down to serious business. No more nice little things just to make life pleasanter at home or to amuse his friends. It was time for him to invent something that would make a difference in the world. It had to be something that would matter to kids, of course.

Thinking about what would make a difference in

other kids' lives took up a lot of Burton's time. When Burton thought, he became absentminded.

One morning at breakfast, Burton's father was so busy composing his music he didn't notice that Burton had become absentminded. Humming softly, Papa Knockwurst let his spoon lie in his bowl, took out his notebook, and scrawled a musical staff—five lines—in it. On the staff he began jotting quarter notes and half notes and grace notes. "Da-da-DUMMMM," he hummed. "De-da-de dum."

The next thing he knew, he found a spoonful of oatmeal close to his mouth with Little Brother at the other end of the spoon.

"Papa, you've got to eat your breakfast," Little Brother said. "You have to keep your strength up, you know."

"MMM-mmm—de-dum—yes—yes," Papa muttered, opening his mouth. He went on filling his notebook with music while Little Brother fed him his breakfast.

"There," Little Brother said at last, neatly patting Papa's chin with his napkin.

Mr. Knockwurst got up from the table and headed for the piano in his studio, a faraway look in his eyes, a pleased smile on his lips.

No. He didn't notice Burton's sudden absent-mindedness.

Nor did Mama Knockwurst. She was thinking of ideas that nobody in the whole world had ever thought before, scribbling numbers in her own notebook. "Aha!" she said, looking pleased. "That's it. The sum of the whole . . . doubled and squared. Yes! I have it! I will have to factor pi into that, of course. . . ."

She pushed back her chair and wandered away toward her laboratory, still talking mysterious numbers to herself.

Little Brother ran after her, calling, "You forgot your beeper, Mama, to remind you to eat lunch."

"Why, aren't you sweet, dear!" Mama said, and patted him absentmindedly on the head.

Of course, Big Sister didn't notice Burton's absentmindedness, either. Her flute lay beside her plate, and every now and then she put down her spoon and fingered the flute holes. She was thinking important things about her invention.

Burton, who never, ever forgot to eat, washed down the last of his carrot-prune square with a big swallow of milk. He scratched Clinton behind the ears, gathered up his books, and was halfway out the door when Little Brother ran after him. "Wait, Burty!"

"Huh?" asked Burton, looking down at Little Brother as though he had never seen him before.

5

"Your shoes!" said Little Brother, pointing at Burton's feet. "It's okay to have one orange and one green sock, I guess. They hardly show under your jeans. But you've got two different kinds of shoes on."

Burton looked down at his feet. Well! So he did! One shoe was brown, the kind he wore on Sundays. The other was a sneaker. It had a hole in the toe. "Uh . . . yeah," he said. "Thanks, Little Brother."

"Hold it for just a sec, Burty," said Little Brother, and he ran to get a matching shoe for him.

Burton waited on the porch step, thinking. A new kind of school bus? Nah—too big. And not much fun for kids, anyway. He had to think of something that was worthwhile and fun, too.

"Here y'are," said Little Brother, coming back onto the porch. He held out a sneaker.

Burton started to take off his sneaker.

"No, no," Little Brother said patiently. "The other one." He nudged Burton's brown shoe with his toe.

And so Burton took off the brown Sunday shoe and put on the sneaker and went to school wearing matching shoes. It didn't matter that a green sock poked out of the hole in the left sneaker and an orange sock poked out of the hole in the right one.

School. Now that was another matter entirely.

Everyone at home understood perfectly about being absentminded. But—

Miss Tilly Doyle, Burton's teacher, expected people to be on time, with their homework done and their papers neat and correct. And she expected everyone to pay attention to every single word she said. All of which was okay for most kids. But it was hard on a boy like Burton, who had inventions on his mind.

Burton settled into his desk and did a page in his science workbook. Then he happened to look out the window, up at the blue March sky. Puffy white clouds were blowing around up there. One looked sort of like a huge gorilla. Burton studied the clouds, hoping to see one that looked like the skyscraper King Kong climbed in that funny old movie. But the clouds kept shifting and changing. There wasn't a skyscraper—or, for that matter, a straight line— in any of them.

One did sort of look like a strange kind of car, though. He got to thinking how sad it was that kids have to move around in slow motion. If kids could have cars . . . real cars . . .

"Burton?"

Burton didn't hear his name.

. . . they could zip around after school. Maybe they could rally at . . .

"Burton Bell Whitney Knockwurst!" roared Miss Doyle.

That got Burton's attention. Whenever Miss Doyle used his whole name, Burton knew he was in trouble. He tore his mind away from cloud sports cars.

Miss Doyle had fixed him with a gimlet eye, which is another way of saying she was practically drilling a hole through his head bones and looking right into his brain.

"Repeat what I just told the class to do," said Miss Doyle.

Burton thought desperately. What had Miss Doyle been saying? He looked across the aisle. Tish put her hand on her social studies book.

"Uh," said Burton, taking a chance, "you said take out our social studies books and . . . and . . ."

"Turn to page thirty-six," Kevin muttered from behind him.

"And," stuttered Burton, "turn to page thirty-six."

Miss Doyle looked crestfallen, which means disappointed. She hadn't expected Burton to know what she had been saying.

"Well," she said, "at least part of your mind was in this room. Really, Burton, you must stop wool-gathering. You must give your whole attention to our studies. You cannot go through life in a fog, you know."

Burton got the idea that woolgathering and fogs mean the same thing—not paying attention. "Yes, ma'am," he said. And he really meant it.

Miss Doyle sat down at her desk. She slipped off her shoes and wiggled her toes. "All right now, people. Page thirty-six. Jonathan, suppose you tell us what was going on around a certain convention hall on July fourth, seventeen seventy-six."

Burton turned his attention to social studies. But not before he whispered thank-you to good old Tish and Kevin for saving his life. The rest of the day he kept his mind on his studies well enough so that Miss Doyle didn't get on his case again.

Needed:
A Good Idea

Where do ideas come from, anyway? Burton didn't know. They just happened.

Sometimes he saw a problem that cried out for an answer, like poor Clinton's misery. That had resulted in the Automatic Dog-Washing Machine.

Sometimes he just wished things didn't have to be the way they were—like having to make his bed every morning. And so his No-Hands Automatic Bed-Making Machine came to be.

And sometimes his ideas grew out of the things

he seemed to see in snow swirling in the wind or in the shadowy lines of a tree at night.

There were more ideas around than Burton could possibly use. It was only when he saw a really great one that he glommed onto it and set to work. He worked fast, never able to catch up with his excitement.

There was no way Burton could have guessed the astonishing idea that was waiting for him to find it that particular day.

They had all just got sprung from Miss Doyle's high-security prison. Burton was ambling toward home with his friends, glad to be out from under Miss Doyle's gimlet eye. They laughed and talked and traded jokes. Kevin had his lariat with him. He practiced roping tricks as they walked along, tossing a loop onto a fire hydrant here, onto a low bush there. He was pretty good at it.

Suddenly, from behind them, came the rolling thunder of skateboard wheels.

"Coming through," yelled a voice. "Outta my way, snails."

Everybody jumped onto the grass, and Merrill Frobusher, a kid from the upper school, zipped past them on his skateboard. He ollied over a big crack in the sidewalk and rolled away. Merrill was the kind of kid who didn't even yell "thanks"

11

to people who got out of his way.

"Look at him go," said Kevin. His lariat hung limply at his side, forgotten, as he watched Merrill eat up the distance on his skateboard. "Talk about speed!"

"He really handles that thing," said Jonathan. "I bet he could do a loop-the-loop on it if he tried."

Loop-the-loop . . . The words trickled into Burton's head.

He watched Merrill curve into the parking lot at the Pretty Penny Supermarket, step off the skateboard, and flip it up into his arms.

"He's got to be the fastest skateboarder in town," said Tish.

Burton stood there, stuck to the spot. He forgot where he was and who he was with and the time of day. How fast could a skateboard really go? And if it got up to maximum speed, what then? What kind of fancy tricks could it do? What if . . . what if—

Eureka! He had it! What the kids of the world would welcome was a better and fancier skateboard. Maybe something even faster than a skateboard.

The others had moved on. When they realized Burton wasn't with them, they stopped and looked back.

"Hey, Burt," called Jonathan. "You coming? Want to stop at the Big Freeze for ice cream?"

12

"Quiet!" Kevin said reverently. "Look at his face. He's got an idea. Don't bother him now."

Burton didn't hear them. Max speed for a skateboard . . . Well no, it could never go as fast as a sports car.

"We'd better see that he gets home all right," said Tish, going back for Burton. "I mean, when he gets like this he could walk right into a truck."

She plucked at Burton's sleeve. "We'll walk home with you, Burt," she said kindly. "Come on."

So, a faraway look in his eyes, surrounded by his friends, Burton headed for home. They steered him safely across the streets and saw that he turned at the right corners. They got his ice-cream cone for him, too—after they dug the coins out of his pocket. They all knew the kind he liked best.

Once he began eating his ice cream, Burton did sort of come to. Bubble gum ice cream. Yum! His favorite flavor. He gave his cone a long, tasty lick. Burton paid serious attention to food.

The kids left Burton at his house. They gave each other meaningful looks as they watched him head up the driveway. The looks meant, "Our genius is at it again," and "What do you suppose he'll invent now?" and "Wow! Are we gonna be surprised!"

Burton didn't go straight to his workshop in the garage. He made a detour into the kitchen. There he put together a sandwich of peanut butter, chicken, avocado, chowchow relish, and a few other interesting things. He took a quart of milk out of

the refrigerator. Then, almost sure he had enough to keep him alive until dinner, he headed toward the workshop.

His skateboard hung on a hook on the wall where it had rested since last fall. He had put it aside in favor of skis and snowshoes and ice skates during the winter. Now, he took it down and set it on his workbench. Munching on his sandwich, thinking *speeeeed*, he studied it.

He remembered where every nick and scratch had come from. They meant that he had become a pretty good skateboarder. Fun! Reaching out, he rolled the skateboard back and forth, remembering the thundering feel of the wheels under his feet as he rolled along the sidewalks. Thunder. Mmmm. That might mean drag on the wheels. Maybe they could be improved. The deck, too—tilt the tail a bit more, round out the nose.

He couldn't use this board. That was clear. It was outmoded.

He returned it to its hook and poked around among the good stuff on his workbench. There were chunks of wood, pieces of metal, and squiggly-looking wires from things he had taken apart. There was a cupcake pan, some shoes, a seatbelt from a car, and some small cans of paint. There were light bulbs of every size, springs, wire cutters and crimpers and benders, wheels of all kinds, bits of rubber, neatly wound rolls of wire and string, pieces of cork—not made of plastic, but the real kind, from trees—spark plugs, capacitors, and lots more.

Yes, there was enough here to get started.

He finished off his sandwich, gulped milk straight from the carton in a manly way, wiped his mouth on the back of his sleeve, and got down to work. He coiled a bunch of wires around a metal tube and studied it thoughtfully. He lined up wheels of different sizes and considered them for some time. Then he pushed everything aside, got out a pad of paper and his marking pens, and began to draw.

Outside, Tish and Kevin and Jonathan crowded around the window.

"Now what's he doing?"

"Making a picture of something."

"What? What is it?"

"Can't see."

"If he's drawing already, maybe he'll begin work tomorrow and then we can see."

The Knockwursts' back door banged.

"Run! Someone's coming."

They scrambled out the gate and into the alley as Clinton came bounding to find out who had invaded his yard. He scratched at the closed gate, barking.

"You want to go for a walk, Clint?" asked Little Brother. "Is that what you're trying to tell me? Or did you just see a rabbit run under the gate?"

Clinton was big on rabbits. He was their mortal enemy.

"Come on," said Little Brother. "We won't chase bunny rabbits. But we'll go for a walk." He opened the gate and Clinton skidded into the alley.

He stopped, looking both ways. No rabbits. No anybody. The alley was deserted. The kids had all disappeared into their own yards.

Inside the workshop, Burton sat back and inspected his drawing. He smiled at it. It was a good working plan. Of course, there would be changes as work went along. The invention would grow into something even better than he had here. He was sure of it.

Yes, sir. What the kids of the world really needed was a new, improved, really fast . . . skateboard? Would it actually be a skateboard when he finished?

"Zoom," Burton said softly. "Zooooom."

16

3

Little Brother in Charge

"What's for dinner?" *Little Brother asked that evening.*

"Mmm-mmm," said Mama Knockwurst. She didn't look up from the thick book she was reading.

"Mama," Little Brother said in a louder voice. "What are we having for dinner?"

Mrs. Knockwurst heard him. "Corned beef and cabbage," she murmured. "Isn't that nice?"

"Mama," said Little Brother, "we can't eat corned beef and cabbage again. We've had corned beef and cabbage every single night this week."

"Have we, dear?" said Mama, looking up from her book.

"We have," said Little Brother, who never forgot anything.

"I don't seem to recall," said Mama. Then she smiled brightly. "But you do like corned beef and cabbage, don't you, dear?"

"Mama," Little Brother said patiently, "if we don't eat something else and get some other kinds of vitamins, our ears are going to fall off."

Mama looked alarmed. "Oh, dear! I wouldn't like that to happen. You children all have such pretty ears."

"So I think we'd better order in," Little Brother said firmly. "I think it would be good to eat spaghetti tonight."

"If you think so, dear," said Mama. "I mean, if it keeps you children's ears on . . ." She went back to her book.

Little Brother took care of everything while Edisonia played her harp-flute. Edisonia gave a little concert every evening. Mama and Papa thought that music was part of living graciously. And she enjoyed doing it. Little Brother listened while he did everything that needed doing.

He ordered the spaghetti and a salad, too. Then he set the table in the dining room with a red-checked cloth and big red napkins and poured the

18

milk. When the doorbell rang, he paid the delivery man with money from the encyclopedia *E* volume. The Knockwursts' household money was safe in the *E* volume. A robber would never think to look under *E* for money. A robber might look under *M* for Money, or *H* for Household Money. But a robber would never think to look under *E* for Extra Money.

Little Brother called everyone to the dining room and went to the kitchen to open the cartons of spaghetti.

Everybody sat at the table and tied on their napkins and waited for him to bring the food.

Mama glanced at the kitchen door. She looked worried. "Dear," she said softly to Papa, "sometimes I fear that Little Brother isn't our child at all."

Papa looked alarmed. "Not ours! Why do you say such a thing, my love?"

"He doesn't act like a true Knockwurst," said Mama. Her forehead wrinkled as she thought. "He is so . . . so . . . in charge of everything."

"True." Papa bit his lip, considering. "And he hasn't invented one single thing. Nothing at all. And he is getting up there—almost eight, isn't he? Do you suppose"—he gulped—"the hospital gave us the wrong baby?"

"Oh, dear!" Mama's eyes filled with tears. Then a tender look crossed her face as she recalled a long-ago day. "When they brought him to me in the hospital, he had on a dear little necklace of blue beads that said 'Baby Knockwurst.' "

Papa cheered up. "There now. See? He must be ours. You have nothing to fret about. And he does, after all, have the Knockwurst freckle." All of the Knockwursts had the freckle, a single freckle, above their left eyebrow.

Mama lost her worried look. "Oh, that is surely the final proof."

"This—this in-charge-of-things trait must be a stage he's going through," Papa decided. "He will outgrow it, perhaps when he gets into middle school. Don't you worry, my love."

And then they turned their attention to the enormous platter of spaghetti Little Brother was bringing to the table.

The spaghetti was perfect. The pasta was al dente, which means it was exactly right for biting into. And the sauce was perfection. It tickled the tongue and made the eater look forward to the next bite.

Burton was glad to be eating spaghetti for a change. But after he got used to the deliciousness of it, his mind went back to his new invention.

This skateboard—if that's what the invention turned out to be—was going to take lots of thought. It would have to go faster than any skateboard ever had. Faster than if a foot pushed it. Faster than going downhill. And, what would a really fantastic skate-

20

board do that the regular kind could not?

Burton only stopped thinking about the skateboard long enough to check the newspaper for garage sale ads.

Burton dropped in on every garage sale in town. That's where he found most of the great things on his workbench. Who knew what use they would be put to someday?

Tonight, as he was writing garage sale addresses in his notebook, he came across another kind of ad. It wasn't like any ad he had ever seen in the paper. It said:

What do you need to know?
Let me tell you all about it.
Knowledge of all kinds.
Clear. Helpful. No charge.
Write to Professor Savvy
Box 1502
Main Post Office.

Now didn't that sound interesting! An inventor never knew when he might need information. It would be neat not to have to stop work on whatever and go to the library and spend hours digging things up. And Burton liked the part about "No charge."

He cut out the ad and tucked it in his notebook for future use.

☰4

Genius at Work

In the days that followed, Burton lived and breathed *invention.* The deck was pretty easy. He got the shape right, the nose rounded, and the tail tilted at just the right angle. Then he was free to think about the wheels.

He tried them small—really small—and he tried them big—really big. The tiny wheels were not efficient. They had to revolve too many times for the distance they traveled. And the really big wheels made the board hard to handle.

At last he got the size of the wheels exactly right. He mounted them on the board, set the board down on the floor, and nudged it with his toe. He watched it roll across the floor. Something . . . something still needed doing. The wheels were noisy. The noise meant a certain amount of drag, and that of course slowed down the skateboard. What to do?

He removed the wheels and sat at the workbench, fingering them, making them spin.

Ball bearings? Was there something he could do about those?

He set the wheels aside, got out his drawing pad, and began to sketch. When he finished, he had a design for ball bearings that were different from any ball bearings anywhere in the world. Someday Burton was going to be famous for those ball bearings. They would come into worldwide use. But for now, they were just for the skateboard.

He made them, put them into the wheels, put the wheels back onto the board, and set it on the floor. The wheels moved without a sound.

And smooth? Were they smooth! A summer breeze wafting over a field of daisies was rougher than those wheels. Those wheels wanted to roll even when they were resting on the perfectly flat workshop floor.

The model looked pretty good. Even without

paint and decorations, it had an unmistakable flair. Look at *me*, it seemed to say. And yet. And yet. It just did not measure up to the wonderful machine that skidded around in Burton's imagination. The model lacked something.

Burton sat there eyeing the invention, ruminating—which means he was chewing over ideas.

It wasn't right. Not yet. He couldn't call it finished.

Would he know when the invention was exactly right? Finished? Perfect? Burton was certain he would. He had a special sense of what was right or wrong with the things he invented. That particular sense sat in his middle somewhat to the left of his belly button, and when an invention measured up to what he had in mind, Burton felt the absolute rightness of it in his middle. It sort of tickled and made him smile.

That had not happened yet with the skateboard. But Burton knew it would. He trusted his sense of the rightness of things as his inventions took shape. He listened to what his "middle" had to tell him.

While Burton was doing all his tinkering, he still had to go to school every day. And that was far from easy. Because Miss Tilly Doyle was not an easy teacher. Take the matter of his handwriting.

24

"Burton Bell Whitney Knockwurst," Miss Doyle boomed on the day she chose to make a big thing about that problem. "How do you expect to show yourself to the world as an educated person, someone to be taken seriously, if people can only read every third word you write?"

How? How indeed!

Burton felt bad. The world would never, he decided, take him seriously. He wanted the world to see that he was a serious person. But it was not going to happen. There was nothing he could do about his terrible handwriting.

He was sorry that he always fell below Miss Doyle's hopes for him.

Miss Doyle went to her desk and sank into her chair. She kicked off her shoes and rubbed her left foot against her right foot. She looked around the room. "All of you could improve your handwriting. Let's take out paper and pencils and do a few handwriting exercises. Burton?"

Burton was staring out the window. Look at those big, fat buds on the trees! Spring was almost—

"Burton! Paper and pencil, Burton. Bur-ton!"

Burton came to. He scrabbled around in his desk, found paper, dug out a couple of pencils, and started his exercises. He looked at the pencil in his hand. Was there some gadget that could help a kid with perfectly terrible writing? Maybe if—

"Burt!" Tish hissed. "Don't go off again."

Burton went to work on his handwriting the old-fashioned way. He practiced. He made rows of *M*s that almost matched. Next he worked on *L*s. Then on *P*s. He kept his mind on it. He used up stacks of paper, really trying, for poor Miss Doyle's sake.

Control, that's what was needed. Control. Maybe a little gadget that would slip onto a kid's finger and . . . A new invention was halfway born.

Suddenly a wayward wind slipped in through the open window. It picked up the papers on the desks and blew them around the room.

Everybody dived for their papers.

Not Burton. He sat watching those papers slip around on the wind, lifting, gliding, settling to the floor.

Now wasn't that wonderful! Those papers moved as effortlessly as—

That was it! He had it! He knew what the invention lacked. He knew what he was going to do that would make it like no other skateboard in the whole world.

A voice cut through his thoughts.

"Burton Bell Whitney Knockwurst," moaned Miss Doyle. She lowered her head into her hands. "Kindly," came the muffled words, "pick up your papers from the floor. And pay attention to your handwriting exercises."

Miss Doyle was at the end of her rope.

Poor lady.

Her life was hard.

"Yes, ma'am," Burton said gently. And he kept his mind alert to the very end of the school day. That wasn't too hard, now that he knew what the skateboard needed.

5

The Perfect
Pen Pal

Burton needed to know some more about aero . . . aero . . . something or other. About how things flew. Big jet planes flew one way and small propeller planes flew another way. Helicopters were quite another matter. And then there were those big air-craft that moved on layers of air. What were they called? Hovercraft? He didn't know a thing about Hovercraft.

He sighed and looked around the workshop. He felt comfortable here, like a bird in its proper nest. But he was going to have to take himself away from the workshop and head for the library. He was going to have to spend days and days reading all about how things flew.

Well, what had to be done, had to be done. Maybe he could fit some of the library time in and around his garage sale visits. He opened his notebook to see which sales were closest to the library. That's where he would start.

As he flipped through the pages, a newspaper clipping fluttered to the floor. He stopped and picked it up. "Knowledge of all kinds," it said. "Clear. Helpful. No charge. Write to Professor Savvy."

Hey! There was his answer! He had forgotten about the ad in the paper. Professor Savvy could save him a lot of time.

He sat down at once and wrote a letter. He wrote

slowly and carefully. He didn't want the professor to read only every third word.

Dear Professor Savvy,
I need to know how things fly—not high, but what keeps them up in the air. How do they get off the ground? Why do they go forward instead of backward? And when they come down, why don't they land hard, with a big thump? Kindly tell me about all this as soon as you can.
Yours truly,
B.B.W. Knockwurst
P.S. It is very nice of you not to charge for doing this.

He reread the letter carefully. He liked the *kindly* instead of *please*—it sounded very grown up. The P.S. was a good grown-up touch, too.

He put dots above all the *I*s and checked to be sure his *A*s looked like *A*s and not *O*s. Then he took the letter to the mailbox on the corner.

When he came home, he stocked up on food from the kitchen—a bowl of kumquats, a box of crackers—and headed back to the workshop. He perched on his stool and ran a finger along the tail of the skateboard. Did it still need a little more tilt?

No, better not mess with it. Now and then he bit into a kumquat or popped a cracker into his mouth.

Eating, looking at the skateboard, he fiddled with a small object, tossing it from hand to hand. From time to time he glanced down at it as though surprised at seeing it there and used a tiny screwdriver to tighten or loosen something.

Suddenly his attention zeroed in on what he was doing. The object had a transistor about the size of a fly's eye and a battery not much bigger. He made sure they were securely in place and screwed down the hatch. There!

He poked around at the back of the workbench and found a box filled with rings. He tried them until he found one that fit his left pointer finger—Burton was left-handed—and soldered it to the gadget. Then he slid it onto his finger.

It throbbed a little against his finger. The feeling

was kind of nice—the feeling you got from touching a purring cat. He reached for a pencil and paper and wrote his favorite words in all of inventing history: "Mr. Watson, come here. I need you."

He leaned back and looked happily at what he had written. It was perfect. The capital letters were all the same height. The *E*s were round and clear. The *M* had perfectly matching humps.

He smiled a contented smile and set the Perfect Pen Pal on the workbench. Miss Doyle was going to be really happy at last. Never again would she have to roar at him about his terrible handwriting. She would be able to read every single word he wrote.

Suddenly he thought of Tish and Jonathan and Kevin. Was it fair for him to have perfect handwriting while theirs was still terrible? No, it was not. If Miss Doyle didn't roar at him, she would roar at them.

He had to be fair.

Well, the problem wasn't one he couldn't solve. He would just put together three more Perfect Pen Pals tonight. He would give them to the kids tomorrow.

He filled his pockets with the makings of the Pen Pals. He covered the model of the invention to keep it secret in case any other inventors happened to pass by and look in the window. Then he picked up the empty kumquat bowl and the empty cracker box and headed into the house.

He put together the extra Pen Pals during Edisonia's before-dinner concert. Or at least he started to. As things worked out, he couldn't give them his complete attention.

Edisonia played "Annie Laurie" on her harp-flute. "Isn't she lovely when she plays," Mama murmured to Papa. "Her neck is so swanlike."

Edisonia went on to "My Old Kentucky Home" and "Believe Me If All Those Endearing Young Charms." Her forehead began to pucker.

Papa didn't notice. "Our Edisonia is not only a fine musician," he said in a low voice to Mama. "She is an inventor the world will hear from."

Playing "Waltzing Matilda," Edisonia bit her lip, looking more and more worried. She ran her fingers along the harp strings in a glissando of sound that ended in a shrill *pinnnnng* and an earsplitting *phweeeeet*. "It's all wrong," she moaned.

"My dear, you are so pretty when you play," said Mama. "The dimples in your elbows are simply fetching. What can the matter be?"

"Tell Papa," said Papa.

"Oh dimples!" said Edisonia, making it sound like a bad word. "At first I thought the harp-flute was

33

just right. But now I know it isn't. They are supposed to sound at exactly the same time. Like this." She blew into the flute and plucked a string. They sounded together: *Pinnnnnng.*
Phweeeeet.

"Now listen," she said. "When I put it on automatic, the flute always follows the harp. It's a teeny bit late. It's not exactly right. Like this."

Pinnnnnng.
Phweeeeet.

She looked terribly, terribly unhappy.

"Mercy me," said Papa, who could not bear to see one of his children unhappy. "Gather around, all. We must help Sister."

So instead of having the rest of the concert, they spent the time thinking of ways to make the harp and flute play at the exact same instant.

"Suppose you play the flute and let the harp be the automatic part," suggested Little Brother.

Edisonia shook her head. "The harp has more strings than the flute has holes. It wouldn't work."

There was no mistaking it, she did know her instruments.

Burton was thoughtful. "Can you make the harp sound come through a loudspeaker? Put a delay in it. Then the sounds would come together."

"But they wouldn't be pure," wailed Edisonia. "It would be a mechanical sound."

34

The long and the short of it was, they didn't find an answer for Edisonia. She was going to have to do more work on her invention. And Burton ended up finishing the Perfect Pen Pals later that evening, sitting on the floor next to his bedroom window, working in the moonlight.

6

Mysterious Professor Savvy

"*My goodness, Burton,*" *Miss Doyle said a few days* later, holding up his book report. "I can read every single word of this. It is beautifully written."

Burton glowed. It was really nice to hear Miss Doyle saying something good to him.

She went on. "You have made remarkable progress with your handwriting. A little old-fashioned practice does wonders."

Miss Doyle was sitting at her desk, going over the class's book reports. She had slid off her shoes, as usual, and was rubbing the toes of one foot against the toes of the other.

Everyone in the class was busy working on private projects.

Jonathan was writing to the government to find out what he should study to get to be an international spy when he grew up.

Tish was drawing pictures of karate movements. She had been going to karate class for two years and was pretty good at it.

Kevin was reading about speed and what it took to break the sound barrier. He was beginning to come out of his cowboy stage. Cowboys were okay. But now he knew what he really wanted to be someday—a race car driver, or maybe a test pilot.

Burton's desk was piled with library books on flying. He was making drawings of propellers. Arrows showed which way the wind went.

The classroom was silent except for the rustle of pages turning and pencils scratching on paper.

A sound broke the silence.

"Ha-rumph!" said Miss Doyle.

It was definitely not a good ha-rumph. Everybody looked up.

Miss Doyle was frowning.

"HA-RUMPH!" There was no mistaking it. That ha-rumph meant business.

Everyone shuddered.

Miss Doyle glared toward Burton's side of the room.

Everyone on the other side of the room slid down in their desks, trying to be invisible.

"What is going on here?" Miss Doyle slapped down four book reports side by side on her desk. "Burton. Jonathan. Kevin. Letitia. Come forward, if you please."

Burton and the others went to stand in front of her desk.

"Who wrote these papers?" Miss Doyle demanded, fixing each of them in turn with her gimlet eye.

"I did, Miss Doyle," they answered in a single voice. It was the truth.

"Do you think I was born yesterday?" roared Miss Doyle. "Somebody is trying to pull the wool over my eyes. These reports"—she stabbed at each of the papers with her finger—"were all written by the same person. They are exactly alike. The Ds are the same. The Ws are the same. So are the Ts and the Bs and every other letter of the alphabet."

Oh.

Burton hadn't thought about that, about the handwriting all looking the same. He had tried to be generous by making the Perfect Pen Pals for his friends. He had thought he was doing a big favor for everybody. Now they were all in trouble because of him.

"Well?" roared Miss Doyle.

Why, he had even thought he was doing a big favor for Miss Doyle by making the kids' handwriting easy to read.

Kevin and Jonathan and Tish turned pleading eyes on him.

"Honest, ma'am," he said. "We each did our own book report."

Miss Doyle's face got red. She looked ready to explode.

Burton dug around in his pocket and held out his hand, palm up. On it lay his Pen Pal.

"Go on," Miss Doyle said in a heavy, I'm-waiting sort of voice.

"I invented this, ma'am," said Burton. He went on to explain about wanting to make his terrible handwriting better, and how he invented the Pen Pal, and how he thought it would help other kids, too.

Miss Doyle listened to the end. Then she closed her eyes and looked patient. She puffed out her cheeks and let out a big breath of air. "Burton, if only you would stop trying to do things the easy way. If only you would buckle down to your handwriting exercises, you would not need a gadget like that."

Burton hung his head. What else could a boy do when his teacher said that to him?

"Ma'am?" said Tish. She looked scared. She also looked as though she had something to say and was going to say it no matter how hard it was.

Miss Doyle fixed her with her gimlet eye.

Tish cleared her throat and licked her lips. "It isn't just a gadget. The Pen Pal is a really good invention. And Burton was really smart to think of it. And—and—"

"And?" said Miss Doyle, her voice rising.

"And it was nice and friendly of him to share it with us," Tish added.

Miss Doyle was surprisingly quiet for a moment. Then, "Yes," she said, "to all of those things. But before this year is over, we will see whether Burton can't invent another use for this 'Pal.' For now"— she took a deep breath—"I say you will learn to write so that I can read your writing. Today, you will all stay after school and redo your book reports in your best cursive writing. There will be no help from gadgets—er, I mean inventions."

That's how it happened that Burton wasn't home that afternoon when Professor Savvy came to see him.

Professor Savvy was a small man with a very bushy mustache and ears that were, one can only say, a true distinction. Nobody should have ears that big.

But Professor Savvy did. Maybe they helped to keep him cool in hot weather, the way a desert fox's do.

He came bouncing along Petunia Street. Anyone watching might almost have said he was skipping. But of course a professor would not skip! He slowed as he passed each house, looking at the numbers beside the doors. At the Knockwurst home, he stopped, smoothed his mustache with a finger, and went briskly up the walk. He mounted the steps and rang the doorbell.

Nobody answered. Edisonia's practicing drowned out the sound of the bell. She was doing something to "The Last Rose of Summer," working it out on the harp-flute. The beautiful melody was interrupted with peculiar unharplike, unflutelike *thungs* and *twiddles*.

Professor Savvy waited, listening and saying "Hoo-haaa" softly when an especially strange sound reached his ears.

Little Brother saw him when he came home from

taking Clinton for a run in the park. "Looking for someone?" he asked, hanging onto Clinton's collar. The long little dog seemed to want to jump on the stranger on the porch.

The visitor smiled cheerily at the small boy who stood before him trying to control his weiner dog. "I am Professor Savvy, come to see the eminent B.B.W. Knockwurst." He bowed from the waist and offered his business card.

Little Brother wasn't used to being bowed to, and he wasn't quite sure what to do—except to hang onto his dog. What was wrong with Clinton today?

"If you will take my card to the eminent Mr. Knockwurst?" said the professor.

Little Brother was surprised. Eminent. That meant *famous*. Papa was eminent, true. But he never talked to people who came looking for him. "You want to see Papa?" Little Brother said doubtfully. "Well, gee, I don't know. . . ."

"Ha-hooo," chortled Professor Savvy. "I assure you he will want to see me. I have here a letter from him." He whipped out Burton's letter and waved it under Little Brother's nose.

Little Brother only had to glance at the handwriting. "Oh, you don't want to see Papa," he said. "You want to see my brother. Burton is B.B.W. Knockwurst, too."

The professor's shoulders sagged. "Hooo," he said

42

softly, sounding rather like a balloon losing all its air. "I came here expecting to talk to a—hoo-hee—colleague, my equal, an original thinker."

"Oh, Burton's original, all right," Little Brother said cheerfully. "He's an inventor."

The professor's face brightened.

"Everyone around our house invents," said Little Brother. A thoughtful look crossed his face. "Almost everyone, I mean."

Professor Savvy gave a happy little bounce. "Kindly take me to your eminent brother," he said. He looked down at Clinton. "Nice doggy," he said. "Be so kind as to remove your teeth from my pants leg."

Little Brother tugged on Clinton's leash. "Burton's not home yet. But he'll be here pretty soon. You can't miss him if you wait here."

Professor Savvy sat down on the steps and was treated, while he waited, to "The Stars and Stripes Forever."

"Ha-hooo," he murmured to himself. "Someone in there ought to tell the flutist to pick up the beat. He's not keeping up with the harpist."

Little Brother looked at Burton's visitor for a long moment. Then, hauling Clinton after him, he went around to the back of the house. He leaned against the workshop door, his arms crossed, still hanging onto Clinton's leash.

≡7

Burton's Pals Hatch a Plan

S*taying after school and doing his book report again* was bad enough. It would have been even worse if Burton had known that all that aero-whatever stuff was sitting on his front steps waiting for him.

One by one, Tish and Jonathan and Kevin handed in their book reports and left, looking back at Burton as he slaved away at his desk. They waited for him on the steps outside school, hatching a plan to find out exactly what he was inventing. Asking him, as they well knew, was no help at all. Burton never talked about his inventions until they were completely finished.

Looking in the workshop window had gotten them nowhere. And after that first day, they hadn't been able to get near the workshop again. Clinton had developed a suspicious streak. He wouldn't let anybody in the yard.

The best they had been able to do was keep track of the books Burton borrowed from the library. Lately there had been books about flying on his desk. Was he building an airplane? But that could not be—airplanes had already been invented.

They had decided to come at the problem sideways.

"See, we'll just sort of ask him cool questions that aren't about inventions," said Kevin, twirling his lasso. "Later we'll add up whatever he says, and maybe we'll have the answer."

So that was their plan.

When Burton came out of school, they all headed homeward together.

"Look, you guys," he said, "I sure am sorry I got you in trouble. I never thought about all of our writing looking the same."

"Aw, that's okay," said Jonathan. "It kept Miss Doyle on her toes."

"You meant to do us a favor," added Kevin, "and that's what counts."

Tish looked thoughtful. "I guess you're going to have to come up with an idea for how to use the Pen Pal. I mean, one that Miss Doyle likes. The invention is too good just to throw away."

"Say, maybe we can get some ideas," said Kevin. He glanced sideways at Tish and Jonathan. "I mean, we can think about that while you work on whatever it is you're inventing right now."

"Gee, thanks," said Burton.

"Are you going to be working for a long time on your new invention?" Tish asked innocently.

"Dunno," said Burton. "It all depends on . . . when . . ."

The three leaned forward. Here it came! A clue!

"On when?" Kevin said encouragingly.

Even as they watched, Burton's face settled into its closed-up look. He was gone. No longer with them. Off somewhere in space where whirling winds lifted things. Maybe . . . maybe . . . a small pair of wings that would slide out from the sides of the skateboard—

A rumbling and thumping came from behind them.

"Outta my way, turtles," called a sneering voice.

Groaning, they jumped aside, with Tish dragging on Burton's sleeve.

Merrill Frobusher thundered past them on his skateboard.

46

"You know," said Jonathan, watching him disappear down the street, "that guy is getting kind of annoying."

"He sure thinks he's big stuff," said Tish.

"I wonder how fast he can make that thing go," Kevin said thoughtfully.

Burton had been jarred out of his thoughts. He wondered, too. Ten miles an hour? Twenty? Well, one of these days old Frobusher was going to see speed that would knock his socks off.

They didn't stop for ice cream because nobody had any money. They all had to rely on whatever was at home in their kitchens and were in a hurry to get there. They didn't lollygag around. They dropped Burton off first and went their separate ways.

As he headed up the driveway, Burton wasn't thinking of anything but a tasty mashed Boston baked bean sandwich and a long drink of cream soda. He was stopped in his tracks by Little Brother and Clinton coming from the workshop and by Professor Savvy stepping off the porch.

"Hey, Burt," Little Brother called. "You've got a visitor. Clinton and I have been hanging around the workshop, sort of keeping an eye—"

He glanced at the professor and didn't finish.

Clinton didn't seem to know whether to growl at the visitor or give Burton a warm welcome home.

47

He did a little of each, growling and wiggling happily at the same time.

"Ha-hoo," said Dr. Savvy, bouncing toward Burton. "I am Professor Savvy, here in answer to your excellent letter."

Wow! At last! Now he could move along to the final stages on his invention. Burton's face lit up and he shook the professor's outstretched hand, trying not to stare at his ears. Burton had never met anyone who hadn't grown up to match the size of his ears.

"Glad to meet you, sir," he said politely. He was puzzled. Wouldn't somebody bringing lots of information have it in his pockets or in a briefcase? Professor Savvy's pockets were not bulging. Burton glanced past him, toward the porch. No briefcase rested on the steps.

"Uh," he said, "I'm sure looking forward to hearing about all the things I asked you in my letter."

"Hoo-hee, my boy," said the professor, "you will have to be a little more definite. Can we talk?"

"Well, sure," Burton said agreeably. He headed for the porch. "We can sit right here on the steps."

Thunggg-phweeet came the music from indoors.

Professor Savvy looked pained. "Perhaps there's someplace rather more restful?"

Burton became aware of the musical—or unmusical—background sounds. "I guess it's hard for someone who isn't used to it to think when my sister practices."

"Your workshop, perhaps?" suggested the professor. "You can possibly give me some idea of your, ha-hoo, project? It would help me to help you, you see."

Little Brother had listened to all this very thoughtfully. He trailed toward the workshop after Burton and Professor Savvy, reaching down to pat Clinton every now and then. Clinton certainly did need a lot of calming down today.

Following Burton and the professor into the workshop, Little Brother saw how, in a swift sweeping glance, the professor's eyes took in everything in the place and zeroed in on the sheet-covered model on the workbench. His eyes glittered, lingering on the model.

8

Why Do Bumblebees Fly?
and Other Questions

Little Brother thrust Clinton's leash into Burton's hand. "Keep an eye on him for a minute, will you, Burt? He's acting goofy today. And I'll"—he picked up the skateboard, sheet and all—"just get this out of your way and bring you something to drink and maybe some snacks."

He sailed out of the workshop, taking the skate-board with him.

Professor Savvy watched him go, disappointment replacing the glitter in his eyes. His mind seemed to be elsewhere. Then he pulled himself together and dug around in his vest pocket. He pulled out a slip of paper and offered it to Burton. "A small sample, a—hoo-ha—promise, you might say, of the help I will give you."

Burton reached for it. Clinton leaped for it, too. Burton won. He bent down and gave Clinton a good petting. "Quiet, Clint. Why don't you just lie down now?"

Clinton nestled his long body into a curve at Burton's feet.

Burton read the slip of paper. Aerodynamics, it said. The study of the way air acts on things that move.

Aerodynamics—so that was the aero word. But he already knew what it meant, even if he didn't know the word. This wasn't much help.

His forehead puckered. Somehow, he had been expecting something more from Professor Savvy. He looked across the workbench at his visitor. The professor had better know about aerodynamics—because with those ears, if a big wind came along it just might carry him away!

Professor Savvy had been flipping through a small notebook. He came to a blank page, his pen held ready. "Now," he said, "if you will tell me something about your—hoo-heee—project, I will get to work at once."

51

The door opened, pushed by Little Brother, who backed into the workshop carrying a trayful of sandwiches, a pitcher, and glasses. "There was a big plateful of sandwiches in the fridge," he said. "Mama made them. Only Edisonia got there first and all the Boston baked bean ones were gone. These macaroni sandwiches are pretty good, though."

He set the tray on the workbench. "I brought mustard and piccalilli. They'll taste good on the sandwiches. And look—Mama made pea-squash shakes."

He poured the pea-squash shakes into the glasses and took one. Then, because there were just two stools in the workshop and Burton and the professor were sitting on them, he found the only other place to sit—on top of a stepladder. He sipped the pea-squash shake. "Not bad," he murmured.

He perched up there, listening, watching, not saying anything. What went on in Little Brother's head when he listened so intently? Nobody had ever thought to ask.

Burton was hollow with hunger. He was weak, not having eaten since lunch. But he had good manners. He offered a macaroni sandwich to his visitor first.

Professor Savvy held up a hand. "No, no. I could not deprive a growing boy of his after-school snack."

No amount of talking could make him change his mind. He did, at last, accept a glass of the pea-squash shake. He sipped and burped softly.

Burton happily bit into his sandwich. Yes, sir, Little Brother was right. Piccalilli was the final elegant touch on a macaroni sandwich.

"I know better than to ask the details of your—hoo-ha—project," said the professor. He laughed gently. "Inventors tend to be touchy about sharing their professional secrets."

Burton felt really good about that. Professor Savvy certainly was thoughtful.

"But," the professor went on, "I am going to ask you to—er, uh—trust me, my boy. Could you give me a little more information to go on?"

The question hung in the air.

Burton polished off the first of the sandwiches and took a long drink of his shake. He was feeling stronger by the minute. "Well, see," he said, "I need to know how fast a thing has to go before it takes off."

Professor Savvy's ears quivered. He wrote something in his book.

"And," said Burton, "birds' wings flap up and down. But airplanes' wings don't. So, why do planes fly without flapping?"

"Amazing questions." The professor pursed his

lips, writing very fast. He looked up at Burton when he finished, smoothing his mustache with a finger. "I have never thought about that."

"And"—Burton was warming up to his subject, talking as he was to such a helpful, understanding person—"I read somewhere that bumblebees should not be able to fly. I mean, because of the way they're shaped. Only, they do. So—why?"

He thought for a long moment, then said, "I guess it isn't fair to ask you that, because I'm only curious. I mean, it hasn't really got anything to do with the—"

"Yes?" The professor leaned forward. "Hoo-ha," he breathed softly. "The . . . the . . . what?"

"Well, with anything I'm doing," said Burton. "So I guess I shouldn't bother you with that one."

The professor picked up his glass. He was about to sip from it. Then he looked at the peculiar color of the pea-squash shake, winced, and changed his mind. "If I run across the answer, you can be sure I will share it with you. Now, what else do you feel—er-um—trusting enough to tell me?"

Burton got a starry look in his eyes, thinking. If you went faster and faster, when you took off, would you keep getting higher and higher? How high could a skateboard go? He sure didn't want to bump into airplanes coming in for a landing at the airport!

54

"And," he said, "what makes a plane go forward and not backward, like I said in my letter?"

A half smile showed under Professor Savvy's mustache. He was writing rapidly.

From his seat up on the stepladder, Little Brother had been looking down over the professor's shoulder, reading what he was writing. Now, suddenly, he slid partway down the ladder and waved wildly at Burton over the professor's head.

Burton couldn't miss all that commotion. He looked up.

Little Brother drew a quick finger across his throat. Cut it off!

Burton understood. He didn't know why Little Brother was acting that way, but Little Brother generally had pretty good reasons for whatever he did. Well, the professor certainly had enough to get started on his research.

"I guess that's all I can say today," said Burton. "I mean, I have to know more before I can do more—if you see what I mean."

"Indeed, dear boy. Indeed." Professor Savvy looked enormously kind. "I understand what makes inventors tick. But just one more question. How soon will you complete your invention?"

In back of him, above him, Little Brother shook his head furiously.

Burton knew what that meant. "Ohhhh," he drawled, "not very soon, I guess."

Little Brother clapped his hands without making a sound.

"Maybe," Burton went on, "in time for the science fair—"

Little Brother shook his head.

"But maybe not till next fall," Burton added.

"Hoo-ha! You can tell me that later," Professor Savvy said understandingly. He stuffed the notebook into his vest pocket. "I will get back to you soon, dear boy, about the ground-to-air speed and so forth."

"It sure is nice of you to go around helping people like this," said Burton. "Do you do this all the time?"

Professor Savvy smiled. It would have been an angelic smile, but it was spoiled by his mustache. Everyone knows that angels do not have mustaches. "Hoo-hee! It pleases me to be helpful," he said with the air of a perfect person. "It is my joy in life to help others."

Little Brother looked as though he might throw up.

"Well, maybe I can do a favor for you someday," said Burton.

"I am sure you will, dear boy," said the professor, his eyes glittering. "I'm sure you will. Well, I shall toddle off now."

Burton held the door for him.

Hastily Little Brother slid down the ladder, paying no attention to the slivers that poked through the back of his jeans. "I'd better walk you to the front sidewalk," he said. "To keep Clinton from biting you."

"Most kind," murmured the professor. "You are a lovely child. And you," he said, glancing down at Clinton, "are a—hoo-ha—faithful dog."

Little Brother hung onto the faithful dog's leash. He followed Professor Savvy outside and down the driveway to the sidewalk and watched him head down the street.

"Hoo-hee" and "Ha-hooo" drifted back to Little Brother. And Professor Savvy skipped. He did!

Little Brother watched him all the way to the corner.

Clinton watched him, too.

In the workshop, Burton sat on at the workbench, doodling on his sketch pad. What had got into Little Brother, anyway? He sure had been acting funny.

And what in heck had happened to good old Clinton? He had been behaving like an attack dog instead of the friendly little weiner dog he was.

Little Brother came back, bringing the covered model with him. "Listen, Burt," he said, setting it on the workbench and taking off its covering. "I don't think you should tell the professor too much about what you're doing."

"I didn't," said Burton. "He couldn't know what I'm inventing from what I said. And you know, he sure was understanding about inventors not wanting to talk about their work."

"See, that's what bothers me," said Little Brother. "He's too understanding. Hey, look—I've got an idea. I heard what you asked him. Why don't I go look it up for you at the library?"

It seemed like pretty hard stuff for a kid like Little Brother. But Burton couldn't pass up a friendly offer like that. "I'll write the questions down," he said kindly.

"You don't have to do that," Little Brother said softly. "Just keep talking. I'll remember."

So that's how Little Brother got tangled up in the invention. He didn't tell Burton what he'd seen Professor Savvy write in his notebook. Burton had a lot on his mind with this invention. There was no need to worry him.

Little Brother would just take care of everything.

9

Roaring Tilly Doyle

In the following days, life got kind of explosive, so many things happened. At school. At home. Anywhere Burton happened to be.

At school, Tish announced proudly that she had earned her black belt in karate. She proved it, too, when one of the big kids from the upper school tried to take over their soccer game. "Who's gonna make me?" he sneered when Tish asked him to go away.

"I said please leave," Tish told him in her sweetest voice.

He doubled over, laughing.

KIIIII-YAH! The next moment he was flat on the ground looking dazed.

Tish, her hands folded before her, bowed politely. "We'd rather you didn't come back," she said softly.

The big jerk took himself off looking like a hound dog that's just been trounced by a chipmunk.

And he didn't come back, either.

"Wow!" said Burton. "You're terrific, Tish."

Tish turned pink and looked shy. "Aw, come on. Play ball," she said softly.

Everyone talked about it for days. They only stopped when the Man from the Government came to school. He appeared in the classroom one day. He was so big that he filled up the doorway.

"I'm looking for Jonathan Culpepper," the man said, showing an official-looking badge.

Jonathan slid down in his desk, his mouth opening and closing like a goldfish's.

"Jonathan?" roared Miss Doyle. "What can you have done! Step to my desk, if you please."

Jonathan sort of dragged up the aisle. He looked like he had thousand-pound weights in his gym shoes.

Miss Doyle took him by the shoulders and looked him straight in the eye. "Have you done something perfectly terrible, Jonathan?" she asked.

"No, ma'am," said Jonathan. His voice squeaked.

Then Miss Doyle turned to the Man from the

Government. "Since Jonathan Culpepper has not done something perfectly terrible, you can talk to me," she rumbled.

Jonathan scooched around behind her, trying to be invisible.

"You want to build a bomb," said the man. "And you request information on the best ways—"

Jonathan got farther and farther behind Miss Doyle and the Man from the Government had to lean around her to keep him in view.

"—the best ways," he continued, pulling a sheet of paper from his pocket and reading from it, " 'to disable a car and a boat and a plane'?"

"Well now, you just let me see that," said Miss Doyle. She took the paper and read it. "Why," she said over her shoulder, "this is a letter you wrote to the government, Jonathan."

"It says there I'm gonna be an international spy when I grow up," squeaked Jonathan. "I figured I could get a head start by knowing that stuff now."

"I see," said Miss Doyle. She turned to the man. "This is a perfectly reasonable request," she roared, waving the letter under his nose.

The man was big, really big, bigger than Miss Doyle. "Madam," he roared right back, "we cannot have just anybody building bombs and knowing how to disrupt transportation."

Miss Doyle took a step forward. "Jonathan Culpepper is not just anybody," she said fiercely. "He is one of *my* pupils."

The Man from the Government stepped backward. "That may be true, madam. But we cannot be sure he won't, er, misbehave."

Miss Doyle wagged her finger under his nose. "He wouldn't *dare* misbehave. I guarantee," she said, stepping and stepping and stepping as the man moved back, back, back, "that neither this child nor any other child in my class will misbehave. Furthermore, when he leaves this school, he will know everything he needs to know to join your organization and learn all of those"—she sniffed—"peculiar things you will wish to teach him."

"But," said the man, "but—but—we are not recruiting just now."

"Well, you ought to be," scolded Miss Doyle. "Because you won't find a better boy—I mean man—when I finish teaching Jonathan Culpepper." She kept backing the man toward the door. "You may come back here and hire him in a few years. And furthermore, how dare you interrupt our classroom work! Out!" she roared, pointing at the door. "Out, out, out!"

And out the man went. He stood on the other side of the glass door looking dazed.

Miss Doyle opened the door for a parting shot. "If you interrupt us again, I will punish you severely. Do you understand?"

"Yes, ma'am," the Man from the Government replied meekly.

Miss Doyle turned back to the room dusting off her hands.

"Jonathan," she boomed, "that was not a very sensible letter to write." She waved it. "For the rest of this term we will work on your sensibleness."

"Yes, ma'am," said Jonathan, breathing like a boy again, not a goldfish.

"Before you go home today, you will write one hundred times: I will think before I write letters."

"Yes, ma'am," said Jonathan, heading back to the safety of his desk.

"Jonathan?"

"Ma'am?" He turned to look at her.

"When you are grown up and an international spy, you just see to it that you are on the right and *good* side of things. Or you will have me to answer to," said Miss Doyle in a voice that was only half a roar.

That was the day they all decided Miss Doyle was a great person to have on their side if they ever got in trouble.

They talked about it a lot. Imagine! Roaring Tilly Doyle sticking up for one of them and scaring away that Man from the Government. Imagine!

Other things happened that week, too. Smaller things. Like Merrill Frobusher getting more and more full of himself when he whipped past them on his skateboard. "Here I come, the emperor of speed. Outta my way, worms, or I'll send you back into last week while I head into tomorrowwwww," he yelled as he rolled past them.

All that boasting about speed really bothered Kevin. "If I had a sports car," he said through clenched teeth, "I'd rev it up and blow him away with my dust."

They started calling Kevin Kev-the-Rev.

Merrill's boasting made Burton all the more certain the invention had to be something super-extra-special.

It was coming along really well now. At the touch of a button, small swept-back wings sprouted toward the front of it. And he had increased the power of the motor at the rear twice. But still the motor wasn't powerful enough.

He needed more information. You could go only so far without paying attention to the theory, the thinking behind things, or you got yourself in a lot of unexpected fixes.

Professor Savvy had not returned. But Little Brother was working on the project in a whole-hearted way. He spent hours and hours after school at the library.

65

He came in from the library later than usual one day toward the end of that week. Dinner was already on the table and he was just in time to sit down and spread his napkin on his lap. He was excited and began to tell Burton right away what he had found.

"I had to go through a lot of books," he said. "But listen, now: Air is the main gas with which aerodynamics is concerned. The laws of physics state that the pressure of moving gas grows less as speed increases." He was looking out into the air over Burton's head and he sounded like he was reading from a book. "This explains the lift on a wing that has a flat underside and a curved top. Because the flow of air is faster over the top of the wing, the air pressure—"

Burton sat there, staring at Little Brother. He had forgotten to chew. He felt like he was listening to a book talking.

Papa Knockwurst had put down his fork.

Mama Knockwurst's eyes were round. So was her mouth.

"Hey," said Burton, "where are your notes? I mean, didn't you write that down for me?"

"Didn't need to," said Little Brother, taking a forkful of mashed rutabaga with toasted marshmallow on top. "I only have to see it," he said as he swallowed. "Then I remember it."

Papa looked dazed. "Do you understand it, my boy?"

"Well, not exactly," said Little Brother. "Well, maybe—sort of. I mean, I don't have to really understand it. See, I only have to tell Burton about it. He's the one who has to understand it."

Mama looked at Papa over Little Brother's head. Her eyes were shining. "Our boy," she said with quiet pride, "emerging from his phase. You were right, dear. It was only a stage he was going through."

"But of course, my love," said Papa. "He is a true Knockwurst."

"Go on," Burton said to Little Brother.

"—is greater on the underside of the wing and the plane is pushed upward," said Little Brother as though he hadn't been interrupted. "Now—"

"Wait," said Burton. "Let's go out to the workshop and I'll do some figures."

"But Burty," Little Brother protested, "we haven't finished eating."

It was the first time in his whole life that Burton had forgotten to eat. "Oh, yeah," he said, settling back in his chair.

"Ahem," said Papa. "This remembering, this not needing to write things down—have you been doing this only recently, my boy?"

"Oh, no," said Little Brother. "I could always do it. Only you never asked."

"Dear, what else can you remember?" asked Mama.

Little Brother wiped some toasted marshmallow off his chin. "Just about anything," he said.

"Can you recall what people have said?" asked Mama.

"Mostly," said Little Brother. "I mean, if you give me the day."

"Thursday. March twelfth. Seven forty-five A.M.," said Papa, picking a date out of the air.

Little Brother was quiet for a moment, as though he was sending himself back to that day. "Papa, you didn't say much. You just hummed 'Da-da-DUMMMM. De-da-de-dum. MMM-mmm—de-dum—yes-yes.' Mama, you said 'A-ha! That's it. The sum of the whole . . . doubled and squared. Yes! I have it! I will have to factor pi into that, of course.' And I said, 'You forgot your beeper, Mama, to remind you to eat lunch.' And you said—"

Papa had turned pale. "My boy, you must not clutter up your mind with every single word that's said."

"Why," said Mama, "there won't be room in your head for thinking about good new things."

"Oh, there's no clutter in my head," said Little

Brother. "I only go back and get stuff when I need it. Mama, this rutabaga with marshmallow is really good."

"I'm glad you like it, dear," said Mama. "I made up the recipe myself. I have done some reading and I understand rutabagas are quite good for keeping children's ears on."

Burton had been sitting there. He had not taken a single bite since Little Brother started talking. Little Brother was a genius, a first-class super genius! He had a—what's it called?—a photographic memory. He could remember everything he saw exactly the way it was printed. Moreover, his ears were like a tape recorder—he could recall everything people said.

He, Burton, the big brother in this family, was going to have to pay more attention to Little Brother. He was going to have to help him grow up and use his amazing talents well.

One thing for sure! They were all going to have to stop calling him "Little Brother"!

"Uh, Little Brother," he said, out of habit. He corrected himself. "Uh, listen, Newton—when we're finished eating, let's go out to the workshop and talk some more about this. I'd like your advice."

Little Brother–Newton's eyes glowed like stars. How wonderful to be treated like a big kid!

≡10

Clinton Stalks the Professor

Burton and Little Brother spent the next couple of days together in the workshop. It was the weekend, and so they didn't have to worry about school. Everyone in the house made things as easy as possible for them.

Edisonia woke them up extra early in the mornings so they could get to work. And she waited till the last minute at night to call them indoors to bed.

Mama Knockwurst brought them their meals on a tray.

Papa even took Clinton for his walks so that Burton and Little Brother wouldn't have to interrupt their work.

Burton had discovered that Little Brother was on his wavelength and thought just the way he did about an amazing number of things. The things they talked about—well, no mere ordinary person could possibly understand.

Little Brother did most of the talking, "reading" the pages of the books he called to mind.

Burton listened and listened. Now and then he would say, "Hey, back up there a little way. Say that over again."

So then Little Brother would rewind his mind like a tape recorder—you could almost hear it clicking—and go back to whatever he had been saying and repeat it word for word.

The many things Burton had been wondering about began to sort themselves out. The parts fit together like the pieces of a really good jigsaw puzzle. He became quite Knockwurstian, speaking in bits and pieces the way Mama and Papa did. "Wings . . . okay. Well, maybe not. Maybe I better move them to the back of the board. . . . Mmmm. Stabilizers, I suppose. But they could be smaller if I . . . if I . . ." He didn't finish his sentences but went on muttering about speed and rudders and flaps.

71

Burton and Little Brother accomplished a lot in those two days.

It was hard, on Monday, to stop work and go back to school. But somehow Burton got through the day without too much pain from Miss Doyle and hurried home as soon as school-day torture was over. Tish and Kevin and Jonathan followed at a distance, not bothering him, just seeing to it that he didn't walk into fences or get run over by a semi.

Little Brother was waiting for him in the workshop. He started talking as though yesterday's discussion had not been interrupted, as soon as Burton opened the door. "Airfoils: planes' wings, of course. They are fixed. But other surfaces such as ailerons, elevators, and so forth can be moved so as to—"

"What I really need to know right now," said Burton, breaking in, "is something more about air pressure. Have you got anything on that?"

Little Brother went through the encyclopedia in his head. "Well," he said, "barometric pressure is . . ."

Suddenly Clinton stirred. He plodded to the door and sniffed at it. Then he sniffed all the way around the four sides of the workshop, his nose at the crack where the walls met the cement floor. He spent an especially long time beneath the window, which Little Brother had covered with striped towels

Grrrrrrr

from the kitchen. Then he followed the wall back to the door and let out a growl just as—*thump . . . thump . . . thump*—someone banged on it.

Burton and Little Brother jumped. Who could that be?

Little Brother tossed the sheet over the skateboard, went to the door, and unlocked the big padlock he had put there last week.

He would have peeked out to see who was there, except that the door banged open and Professor Savvy bounced right past him and into the workshop. Just in time, Little Brother grabbed Clinton's collar and held onto him.

"Hoo-ha! Here I am, at your service," said the professor. He didn't even look at Burton. His eyes went immediately to the workbench and the covered model. He waved a handful of papers, all the while staring at the model as though he was trying to see right through the sheet that hid it from view.

"I am, as you see, as good—hee-hoo—as my word."

Little Brother hadn't taken his eyes off him. "We need more room for you to spread out," he said smoothly, and picked up the skateboard and whisked it toward the door. "C'mon, Clinton, let's take this into the house."

Clinton looked from Little Brother to Professor Savvy as though he wasn't sure he wanted to follow orders.

"Clinton," groaned Little Brother.

If Clinton could have sighed, as people do when they don't want to do something but know they must, he would have. But he followed Little Brother.

Little Brother looked back over his shoulder. "There's some of that great pumpki-baga juice in the fridge. I'll bring some," he said.

Professor Savvy watched him, even as he spoke to Burton. "I have our information. Right here. In these notes." He fanned the papers out on the workbench.

Burton sat there, stunned. He had forgotten all about the professor. Once Little Brother—er, Newton—had gotten into the project and begun getting all the information Burton needed, thoughts of Professor Savvy had disappeared from Burton's mind like fog before a brisk wind.

He no longer needed the professor's services. But how could he tell him that? Now that the professor had gone to a lot of trouble and come back with answers to the questions Burton had asked?

Professor Savvy didn't notice Burton's silence. "I, the great Professor Savvy," he burbled, "the best—hoo-hee—friend of inventors far and wide, will show you what I have here."

He began talking about ground-to-air speed, and about how it all partly depended on the size of the aircraft's wings, and about birds flapping. "They can't get enough forward speed, you see, so they must flap their wings to lift themselves."

He was talking about why things went forward, even against the wind, and not backward, when Little Brother returned with the pumpki-baga juice. Clinton almost tripped him, scrambling past him through the door. He headed for the professor.

"Aw, come on, Clint," Little Brother pleaded. "Lie down there next to Burt, will you?"

Clinton would have rolled his eyes if he could have. But he did as he was told.

"Mama calls this pumpki-baga juice," explained Little Brother, setting down a frost-covered pitcher, "because it's got pumpkin pie flavor but there's a whole lot of rutabaga juice in it. That's good for keeping children's ears on, you know." Then he felt himself get red. He was talking to someone with huge ears. He should not have said *ears*. Hastily he poured a glass of juice and offered it to the professor.

Professor Savvy sipped. His eyes watered. His ears quivered. "Very—er-uh—interesting," he said, and set the glass down and went on talking about how high planes could fly, and the differences between jet and propeller planes, and why things didn't land—as Burton had put it in his letter—with a big thump.

Burton listened with growing surprise. He had already found these things out, from Little Brother's reading. It was simple stuff, really—baby stuff. He had gone way beyond it. Why, he knew more about flying than the professor did!

". . . and I trust this is what you had in mind," Professor Savvy said smugly. He looked highly satisfied with himself. "I trust that my hoo-ha—vast research will be helpful to you. And now"—he tapped his open notebook—"now if you will tell me a bit more about your project, I will get on to the next stage of our research."

Burton scratched his head. How could a boy tell a grown-up, especially one who was a professor, that his research was kindergarten stuff? Why, a man like Professor Savvy probably knew all kinds of other stuff that no ordinary person did.

76

He sighed. He was in a pickle. Inventing something nobody had ever thought of was easier than knowing what to do about this problem. But he had to be truthful. He had to be honest. He would try to be kind to the professor.

"This has been really nice of you, sir," he said. "But I can't tell you more because I can't ask you to look up more things." He swallowed. "Because . . . because . . ."

He just couldn't say it! He couldn't tell the professor that his research wasn't worth a rap. Burton licked his lips. "Because I can't tell exactly where I'm going myself," he finished awkwardly.

In a way that was true. Who knew what kind of final touches would happen before the invention was finished?

"You don't know?" The professor sounded disbelieving. He smoothed his mustache with a finger. "But surely the . . . the . . . object I just saw carried out of here under its covering is a little bit bigger? A teeny bit longer? A whole lot lumpier than it was last week?"

Burton didn't answer directly. "I'm sort of . . . kind of . . . flying by the seat of my pants," he said lamely.

Professor Savvy pounced on that. "Aha! So your invention does have to do with flying!"

"I didn't mean that exactly," Burton burst out.

Little Brother spoke up. "Flying by the seat of the pants," he recited. "Another way of saying development of something by instinct or by the mood of the moment. This saying was first used by—"

Professor Savvy ignored him. "Well! Considering the work I have done, the information I have so carefully gathered, the least you can do," he said in high huffment, "is to share with me a bit of what you are doing here."

Burton couldn't do that. He could never talk about an invention before he finished it. If he talked it, then he couldn't do it. He thought the professor had understood that.

"Sir," he said earnestly, "you've been really nice. I hope to do a favor for you someday. I promise I will."

"Burton is a man of his word," said Little Brother. "He keeps promises. He always does."

"Well!" huffed Professor Savvy, snatching his papers off the workbench, "I do not know when I have been so badly treated."

Burton looked miserable. He didn't know what to say.

Little Brother looked puzzled. He didn't trust this professor guy. But he didn't know how to get him out of the workshop.

But Clinton did. He did what was natural to him. He always went after creatures with big ears, although those creatures usually happened to be rabbits. He began to stalk the professor.

Professor Savvy looked down and saw Clinton coming toward him, his pointy nose close to the floor, a low growl coming from his throat. The professor began to back away. He moved more and more quickly.

So did Clinton.

At the door, Professor Savvy turned and ran.

Clinton flew after him, his low middle practically skimming the ground, his stubby legs churning.

Little Brother darted after him, yelling, "Hey, Clinton, don't bite! Don't bite!"

Burton sat on at the workbench, doodling idly on a scrap of paper. He was glum. He was as morose as he could possibly be. He loved inventing things. But sometimes, like right this very minute, when he had hurt somebody's feelings, he almost wished he weren't an inventor. If he weren't an inventor, if he were just like other people, he wouldn't do different things that made people unhappy sometimes—himself included.

Sounds came through the open door behind him. Clinton barking. Little Brother calling. The *plungggg-thweeet* of Edisonia's harp-flute. A truck

passing in the street. A jet plane overhead. A squir-
rel chattering—

Hey, wait a minute!

Burton sat up tall.

Gone were the gloomy thoughts.

He blinked. That was it! He grinned. That was *it*!

Little Brother came back, carrying the skateboard
and hauling old Clinton on his leash.

"Newton," said Burton, "do you happen to have
any information on rockets?"

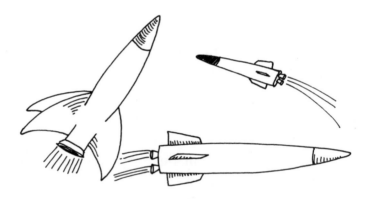

11

Professor Savvy Sulks and Skulks

"Rockets," recited Little Brother, checking out the information he had on hand. "Mmm-mmm . . . discharge a thrust of air, thus producing forward movement." He looked bewildered. "What have you got in mind?"

"What I'm thinking," said Burton, keeping his excitement under control with great difficulty, "is, the board is pretty good right now as it is—"

"But you haven't road tested it yet," said Little Brother in his practical way. "So you don't know that for sure."

"I'll get to it, I'll get to it," murmured Burton. "I'm thinking beyond that. Like . . . the thing that could make the big difference between this board and the regular kind, the thing that could make it take off, would be a little extra power."

"You mean *really* take off?" asked Little Brother, interest lighting his face. "You mean like into the *air*?"

"You've got it!" Burton nodded solemnly. "Not a whole lot, you understand. Just enough to get up high enough to . . . to . . . well, do some really interesting stuff on it."

Little Brother's eyes were round with wonder as he thought about the great "stuff" a rocket-powered skateboard could do. Then the practical side of his nature surfaced once more. "Wouldn't the rockets have to be really small?"

"Uh-huh." Burton welcomed Little Brother's input. Whatever he had to say always made sense. "See if you can find anything on midget rockets."

"How would you stay on the thing?" asked Little Brother. "I mean, what if it zips right out from under you?"

Burton thought about that, biting his lip. "Now that you mention it . . . The rider could fall back into the exhaust and . . . and . . ."

"Get barbecued?" asked Little Brother.

Burton had already moved beyond that thought. "I'll have to invent some kind of grip system," he said thoughtfully. He stowed the idea away at the back of his mind. Later. Later he would think about that part of the problem. "For now, I need to know about rockets. Little bitty ones."

Little Brother headed for the door. "Back to the library," he said.

He looked down at Clinton, who was padding after him. "Burty, you'd better keep an eye on Clinton," he added. "They won't let me take him inside the library."

"Right," Burton murmured absentmindedly, his mind already tuned into the drawings on his sketch pad.

"On second thought," said Little Brother, eyeing Burton's back, "I'll tie him in the yard."

Burton didn't hear them leave. One rocket mounted at the back? Or two, one on each side of the deck? Mmm-mmm . . .

He picked up the model and balanced it on his open palms, studying it. No, he couldn't use just one rocket at the back. The tilt at the rear of the deck would aim the thrust at a slightly upward angle. And that would force the skateboard's tail toward the ground. No. There would have to be two rockets, one on either side, toward the rear, sending their powerful blasts out alongside the board.

He could see it already, himself on it, moving upward into a loop-the-loop.

"Va-room," he said happily. "Va-ROOOM."

He had forgotten all about Professor Savvy and the unhappy meeting of an hour ago.

But Professor Savvy had not forgotten about Burton. He had been—ha-hoo—most shabbily treated by that boy. He was not going to put up with it. No, he was not. The boy was—hoo-hee—definitely onto something. And he, Professor Savvy, the Great, the Magnificent, the Brilliant, was going to find out what it was.

In spite of that pesky little brother.

In spite of that dratted dog.

He had skipped away down the street, casting an eye back at the Knockwurst house now and then. When he sensed he was no longer being watched, he turned the corner and skulked along under the trees. When he came to the alley, he headed back to the garage-workshop. He lurked nearby for the rest of the afternoon, crouching behind the trash cans when anyone came along.

He didn't hear anything except an occasional growl from the dog, which was tied up in the back yard.

What *was* going on inside the workshop? Why did the boy have to be so all-fired quiet about his work! Well, whatever it was, he, Professor Savvy, the Remarkable, was certain that he could do much more with the idea than the boy could. Good ideas should not be wasted on kids!

/Professor Savvy sulked and skulked and lurked for the rest of the afternoon. But to no avail.

All he saw, at last, was Little Brother come home from somewhere or other . . . go into the workshop . . . come out with Burton . . . and fasten a new extra-big super-tough padlock on the door. They headed toward the kitchen door, dragging the dog after them. The professor could hear them talking.

"Come on, Clint. You don't want to go out in the alley. It's dinner time."

"There aren't any rabbits out there, Clint. Clinton Knockwurst, come *on*."

"Did you find anything?"

"Well, sure."

Professor Savvy leaned forward, the better—hoo-hee—to hear what had been found.

"But not enough. I'll have to go back tomorrow."

"Tell me what you did get."

"After dinner. I'm so hungry I could eat a rubber boot fried in suntan oil."

Professor Savvy remembered the pea-squash shake and the pumpki-baga juice. He shuddered to think what the Knockwursts might be having for dinner.

85

Time to go home and dine on something civilized. Creamed eggs on oatmeal, perhaps—real Scotch oatmeal. That's what his dear old granny used to fix for him when he was a small boy having a bad day. Creamed eggs on oatmeal. Such comforting food.

A glissando of harp notes showered out of the house.

Professor Savvy winced, turned, and skipped toward home.

Indoors, Edisonia blew into her flute, testing it. A trilling—almost like birdsong—filled the room.

"Lovely," sighed Mama.

Edisonia combined the harp and the flute. *Plonnggg-phweeet.* The sounds fought against each other. Her eyes filled with tears.

Papa, coming into the room, saw the tears and was filled with sadness. Poor, dear child. Her invention was not going well. But then he remembered and smiled. Today he had news that would dry his little girl's eyes.

"Children," he said. "My love." He bowed to Mama. "I have news."

All eyes turned to him.

He folded his hands across his middle, smiled around at them, and announced, "My new piano concerto is to be played next week by the Kirksville Philharmonic Orchestra."

"No!" breathed Mama.

86

"I am to play it," said Papa. "And"—he turned to Edisonia—"you, dear child, will turn the pages for me."

Edisonia's face shone. Her tears sparkled like raindrops in sudden sunshine. "Truly, Papa? I will be right on the stage beside you? Reading your music? Turning the pages as you play? Oh, Papa!" She whirled around the room on her toes.

"Oh, my dear," said Mama. "What an honor for you! And what a splendid opportunity for our girl. This could not have come at a better time. I have been worried—she is becoming careworn."

"It will take her out of herself," said Papa. "And she won't even have to miss school, since spring break is about to begin."

It wasn't until much, much later that Burton and Little Brother got to talk about Little Brother's findings at the library. They sat on the floor under the windows in Burton's room, in the moonlight. It was after lights-out. One thing Papa and Mama were firm about and never, ever forgot was bedtime.

"Well see," said Little Brother, "I did find out some about rockets. I'll give you that in a minute. But I didn't find anything about how to make them really small."

Burton was thoughtful. "Fireworks are kind of like rockets. Maybe you could try looking up fireworks."

Little Brother hadn't thought of that. "I'll do that

next," he said. Something bothered him, though. "Fireworks always blow up. That's what makes them fun. Only, you don't want the board to blow up. What about that?"

Burton was pleased to see that Little Brother's— er, Newton's—head was really working. "Rockets and fireworks only give me an idea," he explained. "But the thrust will have to happen for as long as I want it to."

That satisfied Little Brother. But he was still troubled. Once he got an idea in his head, he couldn't let go of it. He was like Clinton worrying a bone. "Burty, you've got to road test the invention."

Burton knew the board was okay. He had designed every part of it and was certain it would work exactly as planned, moving swiftly, smoothly, silently. But Newton was just a little kid and new at inventing. He didn't understand that things worked for-sure once you got the theory—the thinking part—right. He was going to have to take the time to set Newton's mind at rest.

"Okay," he agreed. "We'll have to take it out when nobody's around, though."

"Saturday morning," suggested Little Brother. "Real early. The first day of spring break everybody sleeps in."

They left it at that.

≡ 12

The Big Road Test

Little Brother got them up and on their way while the sun was still just a big red ball hanging low in the eastern sky. "No," he said to Clinton, who tried to follow them out the back door, "you can't come with us, boy. You'll get in the way or get run over. I'll come back soon and take you for a walk." He closed the back door on Clinton's whines of protest.

Burton and Little Brother had thought everybody would sleep late that morning. They could not have been more wrong.

The leaves at the top of the butternut tree in the back yard fluttered and rustled when Burton and Little Brother came outside.

The butternut tree practically turned into a quaking aspen when Little Brother unlocked the workshop door. A soft, excited hooo-heee floated down from high in the tree.

Little Brother held the door and Burton rolled out onto the driveway on the model.

The sound from the treetop shifted to a disappointed "haaaa," rather like the air escaping from a balloon. Professor Savvy watched Burton roll toward the street, Little Brother trotting after him.

Drat the boy! He was playing! There was still work to be done on the invention—whatever it was—that waited in the workshop. And what was the boy doing? Taking time out to play! *Play!*

The professor slid down the tree and checked the door. But the extra-big super-tough padlock held fast. He leaned against the wall, pouting. He was only feet—maybe even inches—away from the precious invention . . . separated from it only by a thin wall . . . and he couldn't get to it.

Didn't the boy know there were more important things in life than amusing himself? He was never going to be a first-rate inventor if he dropped his work just like that—the professor snapped his fingers—and took himself off to play.

The boy didn't deserve to succeed. No, he did not.

Professor Savvy sulked until he heard a noise at the back door. Hastily he slid around the side of the workshop and peeked out as the boy's father and sister came out onto the back steps. They were going somewhere, that was clear, for they both carried suitcases.

Well, there was no point in staying here. He might as well keep an eye on the boy. Maybe he would say something that would shed light on whatever he was up to in the workshop.

Silently, the professor slipped into the alley and skipped off in the general direction of the park, which is where the boy seemed to have been heading.

Professor Savvy wasn't the only one up and out that morning. The newspaper delivery boy was out, flinging papers into the bushes at the front of houses. A trash collector was out, rattling garbage cans, emptying them into the back of his big buglike truck and setting its machinery whirring. A diaper delivery service was out. And a dry cleaner. And so was Tish.

Tish spied Burton from halfway across the park. She was on her way to the all-night market to get milk for breakfast. She stopped in her tracks and watched him whiz around the bandstand with a quick shifting of his weight and a lithe movement of his hips. Funny. She had forgotten what a good skateboarder Burton was. She hadn't seen him on his board since last summer.

She walked backward, watching him. But she didn't have time to catch up with him and talk. Everyone at home was waiting. They couldn't eat their cereal until she got back with the milk.

Kevin was in the park, too. He was practicing his roping. He laid a loop on a statue of Hans Christian Andersen, tightened the rope, and walked toward the statue, holding the rope taut as he might have held a roped steer. When he got to the statue he practiced doing a few good knots around Mr. Andersen's feet and ankles.

Of course, it would be a different matter, roping and tying a live, wiggling dogie. But for the moment, he had to work with what was on hand.

As he stood up, looping the rope neatly over his arm, something rushed past him. He looked up and saw Burton's retreating back.

"Hey, wait for me," he yelled. "I'll come, too."

He spoke to the wind. Burton was there and gone, too far away to hear him.

Wow! Kevin watched him with envy. To be able to move that fast! Funny, though. He didn't remember Burt revving up to anything like super speed on his skateboard last summer.

93

Burton passed Jonathan, too. Jonathan was out looking at things that had been left strewn around the park. A ballpoint pen. A candy wrapper. A twist-tie from a plastic bag. Nothing was too small to catch his eye. International spies could tell a lot about people from the clues they left behind.

Take the pen, for instance. It wasn't the cheap kind—it must have cost at least a dollar. So, a grown-up had undoubtedly lost it. He tested it. It still wrote. Thus, it had been lost, not just tossed away. It was black, not red or blue, which meant—

His mind was taken off the owner of the pen by a whooshing wind. Burton glided smoothly, swiftly, past him, Little Brother sprinting at his side. Jonathan started to call out, but his attention was caught by something else.

That guy, dodging behind trees and peering out. He didn't want to be seen, that was clear. Who was he? Strange-looking guy . . . not very big for a grown-up . . . with a bushy mustache and huge ears . . .

Peculiar. Strange. Why was he following Burt?

Tucking the stuff he had picked up into his pockets, Jonathan took off after the stranger. No harm in keeping an eye on the guy. No harm at all. And it would give him another chance to test his spy powers.

Heading for home, Burton whipped back toward the bandstand. "Okay?" he asked Little Brother, grinning. "Did I prove it? Does this machine move or does it *move?*"

"I believe you. I believe you," panted Little Brother. He was beginning to find the pace a little rough.

"So you'll get the rest of the info I need today?" asked Burton, dismounting. He would walk the rest of the way. Newton needed a rest.

"I betcha," said Little Brother, glad to slow down, "I betcha I can get everything you want by the time the library closes today."

"Think," said Burton, "just think. If the board moves this fast now, think what it'll do with a little extra power."

They headed for home.

With Professor Savvy following them.

And Jonathan tailing the professor.

In the distance, Merrill Frobusher stood, hands on his hips, one foot on his skateboard, watching

Burton through narrowed eyes. Where had that Knockwurst kid picked up all that skateboard skill? He hadn't been out, training. Well, then, the skill must be left over from last summer, before Merrill moved to town.

Strange, to be that good at something and never use it.

Merrill pushed off, following Burton.

He was going to have to keep an eye on the kid. After all, he had a reputation to uphold as King of the Board.

Nobody, especially a kid from middle school, was going to take it away from *him*.

13

Tracking Spies

It was downright peculiar, eating breakfast without Papa and Edisonia. Little Brother didn't have anyone to look after. So he settled Clinton in Edisonia's chair and fed him dog biscuits soaked in grape juice. Having Clinton sitting at the table wasn't exactly gracious dining. But Mama didn't even notice. She was busy drawing rhomboids and triangles in her notebook.

Afterward, Little Brother headed for the library to finish looking up the stuff Burton needed, and Burton went to the workshop.

97

He did a quick sketch of the skateboard with the rockets in place, adding wavy lines where it seemed likely to wobble when it picked up speed. He would control the wobble with proper balance. He was certain he could do that. But when the rockets first kicked in . . . He remembered Newton's question about the skateboard zipping out from under the rider.

Doodling idly, thinking about the problem, he found himself sketching Miss Doyle. Her desk. Her kicked-off shoes underneath the desk. Shoes . . . shoes . . .

Suddenly he sat up straight. His thoughts went from low gear into high and then into race. Shoes—that's what was needed. Special shoes that would stick to the deck. Maybe little electromagnets on the board? With bits of iron on the soles of the shoes . . . The electromagnets would have to be controlled by remote, of course, so that the shoes' grip could be turned off and on as needed.

He couldn't do anything more about the exhaust until Newton came home from the library. But he could work on the shoes.

Shoes, shoes, wonderful shoes. He began to hum. Thank you, Miss Doyle. He was going to have to do something special by way of thanks to her. Shoes . . . shoes . . . He lost himself in the project.

He didn't hear anything going on outside in the yard.

The kids had gathered there. Jonathan had called Tish and Kevin and told them to meet him.

"What's up?" asked Kevin, neatly tossing a loop over the yard lamp.

"Did you see Burton on his skateboard this morning?" asked Tish. "I wonder what he was doing. I mean, he hasn't ridden it since last summer."

"Come with me," Jonathan said mysteriously.

Exchanging puzzled glances, Kevin and Tish followed him into the driveway. Jonathan stopped midway between the Knockwursts' and the neighbors' house. There weren't any bushes nearby, no place where someone could hide and listen to them. He began talking in a low, serious voice.

"Somebody's tailing Burton," he whispered, glancing over his shoulder.

Kevin whispered, too. "The Man from the Government?"

"Are you sure they were following Burt?" asked Tish. "I mean, maybe they were just wandering around the park and only looked like they were following Burt."

Jonathan shook his head. "No, it wasn't the Man from the Government. And no, it wasn't somebody who just looked like he was after Burt." He described the weird little man. "He kept ducking behind trees," he finished, "and peeking out, always at Burt, never at anyone else."

Tish and Kevin agreed: You had to wonder about a person who hid behind trees and peeked.

"He followed Burt all the way home," said Jonathan, "and—"

Tish and Kevin leaned forward.

"—and he sort of sneaked around the workshop. Only he couldn't get in because the door was locked."

"The invention!" breathed Tish. "He's after the invention."

"You've got it," said Jonathan. "What else?"

Kevin was for quick action. "We've gotta go tell Burt."

"Hold it!" Jonathan didn't agree. "We don't want the guy taking Burt's mind off what he's doing."

"If Burt gets sidetracked," said Tish, "it'll take him forever to finish and we'll never find out what the invention is."

"What we've got to do," Jonathan said seriously, "is set up a watch. One of us has always got to be here in the yard. That'll discourage the guy. And maybe—well, I'm going to try—I can find out more about him."

So that's what they agreed to do, and they put their plan into action right away. They did their best to look as though they were just hanging out, whiling away their time. They tossed a ball among themselves, lazily, as though there was nothing better to do.

Things were quiet and relaxed. Jonathan kept an eye on the street and the alley.

There was a lot of Saturday morning traffic. Mothers were out with their shopping carts, calling to little kids who scattered like pinballs. Delivery trucks moved along slowly, stopping here and there. Merrill Frobusher rolled past, not going at his usual break-the-limits speed. He glanced into the yard, but he didn't call any insults.

A fat man in a trench coat, his hat pulled low over his face, ambled along the street. Jonathan got the feeling he and the others were being inspected. But the man didn't stop.

Something about him hooked Jonathan's interest, though. What was it? He moved farther down the driveway, the better to see. But he was cool about it, watching out of the corners of his eyes as he called to Kevin, "Put it here, Kev."

Kevin winged the ball to him.

Jonathan caught it, spinning on his toes as he did so—just in time to see the fat man turn the corner.

He tossed the ball to Tish. "Here ya go," he called. In a quieter voice he added, "See you in a little while."

101

Without turning her head, Tish watched him take off down the street. Jonathan was onto something. He sure was good at the spy business.

She and Kevin gave up on playing catch and went to sit on the back steps where they could keep a close eye on the workshop. They traded jokes, waiting for Jonathan to come back. But the jokes didn't work. When Tish started one, Kevin finished it. And when he told one, Tish came out with the punch line. They all knew one another's jokes.

Burton's little brother Newton came home from somewhere and let himself into the workshop. He was in there a long time. After a while, he came out, went into the house, and came back dragging a shopping bag full of knobby, rattly stuff and took it into the workshop.

Sounds came from the workshop. Sizzles and soft pops. Tish and Kevin couldn't be sure whether they saw smoke come out under the door or not. Kevin thought so. Tish didn't.

Eventually Jonathan did return. "Lost him," he said in disgust. "He was wearing a disguise, but I know it was him—the guy I saw in the park."

"What kind of disguise?" asked Tish.

"A raincoat with a belt," said Jonathan. "You know—the kind spies wear. And he looked really fat. He bulged above and below the belt."

102

"Hey, you can't go around being suspicious of every fat guy in a raincoat," said Kevin. "Maybe that's what he really was—just a fat guy in a raincoat."

"With a stomach that kept slipping?" asked Jonathan. "And him having to push it back up in place? I think it was a pillow. It was him, all right."

"Where did he go?" asked Tish. "Did you track him to his"—where did a spy go?—"to his headquarters?" she finished.

"Couldn't." Jonathan looked downhearted. "A whole bunch of funeral cars went past on Persimmon Street. Everybody had to wait. He got across the street before the cars came and I couldn't cross."

"If he came here once," Tish said comfortingly, "he'll come again. You'll catch him next time."

But when they thought about it, none of them was sure whether they wanted the man to come back so that Jonathan could catch him. Because, after all, he meant trouble for their friend Burton.

≡14

Moose Snorts and Hippo Sighs

*Astonishing noises began to come from the work-*shop. Sizzles and pops and hisses and, one morning, a bang that shook the walls.

Tish and Kevin and Jonathan, who hadn't left the yard unguarded since spring break began, jumped.

"Those are fireworks!"

"But why would he set them off inside?"

"Do you suppose he's working on something for the city centennial?"

Skipping down the alley, a little old lady with an

104

unusually fat lip and frizzy white hair that stuck out all around her head, paused, listening. "Ha-hooo," she said softly. "More shenanigans. No work, more play. And," she added, "selfish selfish selfish—setting off fireworks where nobody but himself can enjoy them. Tsk!"

Even Merrill Frobusher, who had taken to riding up and down Petunia Street in recent days, slid to a stop, staring toward the workshop. But he didn't enter the yard to ask about it. Because he hadn't been exactly friendly to anybody there. He couldn't help wondering, though, where the Knockwurst kid was. Why hadn't he been out on his skateboard since Saturday morning?

In the following days, the sounds from the workshop went through all sorts of interesting changes until the bangs—for there were more of those—became less alarming. They began to sound like the grumpy snorts of a moose having a bad day.

The kids had given up trying to guess what was going on. It would, they knew, be something nobody had ever thought of. You can't guess about something you can't even imagine.

But the delivery man in the leather jacket with the collar turned up high around his ears and a hat pulled down low—he wasn't above guessing. Hunched beneath the big carton he carried on his

105

shoulder, he stood in the alley, listening. "Heee-haaaa," he said. "Those are rocket sounds, those are!" He was certain. Whatever the boy was doing in there, it was something that used rockets. And rocket power—aha!—meant something that *flew*!

He was forced to move along, however, when Jonathan came to the gate and looked out into the alley.

The delivery man hoisted the carton higher on his shoulder. Drat that boy and drat his friends! Drat all the nosey-Parker kids who got in the way of great minds at work. Why didn't they find something better to do than hang around the Knockwurst yard?

Grumbling to himself, he continued on his way. But then—thinking "rockets," thinking "something that flies"—he cheered up. Yes, by George, he had begun to have an idea or two! Thinking cheerful rocket thoughts, he couldn't keep a little hippety-hop out of his walk.

Jonathan, leaning on the gate, watched the retreating form of the delivery man. Something stirred at the back of his mind. But he couldn't quite . . . quite . . . pick up on what it was. . . .

Meanwhile, the moose snorts shifted into still another phase. They became quieter, gentler. They began to sound like maybe the moose was settling down for a nap—not an altogether unpleasant noise.

106

But then even that sound changed. It became the contented sigh of a hippopotamus sinking into a clear, cool pool.

On that day, the last day of spring break, as it happened, Burton leaned back, admiring the invention.

There it sat, gleaming with a new coat of paint. It was a smooooth-looking vehicle, all right. He touched a button on the remote, a small box that fit into the palm of his hand. Swept-back wings unfolded on each side of the skateboard, at the rear. Mini rockets sprouted beneath the wings.

Burton grinned. His middle felt wonderfully comfortable—as though he had just polished off a quart of bubble gum ice cream and licked the spoon. It was the unmistakable "good" feeling he always had when something he was working on was absolutely without-question RIGHT.

"Theee end," he said softly. "Done!"

Little Brother, his elbows on the workbench, his chin resting on his fists, said admiringly, "It sure is some skateboard." But then his levelheaded way of looking at things made him add, "I guess you can't really call it a skateboard, though. Not anymore. I mean, with the wings and the rockets and the remote control. What *are* you going to call it?"

Burton tapped the remote. The wings and the

rockets slid out of sight. "It sure looks like a skate-board when I do that," he said. He hadn't thought about a name for it. "It's an invention," he said, "a . . . a . . . machine."

"It's got to have a fancy name," said Little Brother. "You owe it a fancy name. You better think about it."

"No," said Burton, "you think about it. I'm all thunk out."

He was feeling so good about the invention he was ready to explode.

He didn't want to leave it long enough even to eat dinner.

He was so proud of it that he wanted to keep it nearby, where he could admire it. Last thing before he went to bed. First thing tomorrow morning.

Little Brother guessed how he was feeling. "Let's take it into the house," he said. He tossed the cover over it as they got ready to leave the workshop. He took one last look around, gathered up all the sketches, locked the door, and followed Burton toward the back door.

Tish and Jonathan and Kevin were in the yard, of course. They took in Burton's clear-eyed happy-looking face and the sheet-covered something he was carrying.

"It's finished!"

108

"Are you going to let us see it?"

"What *is* it?"

"Yep," said Burton, "I just finished it. And yep, you are going to see it. You'll find out what it is after school tomorrow."

"Awwww," they all groaned.

"Hang out in the school yard," said Burton, "and I'll meet you there."

No amount of pleading would make him tell what it was he carried, hidden under the sheet.

Talking about it would only sound like bragging. People would have to see what the invention could do. They would have to see it in motion. And then they could decide for themselves that it was—spectacular.

"Tomorrow," he said firmly. "After school."

Tish and Jonathan and Kevin dragged themselves toward home. There was no need to guard the Knockwurst yard anymore. The invention would be safe inside the house tonight.

Burton and Little Brother went into the house for dinner.

The door closed—*thud*—behind them.

"Ha-hooo," came a gleeful chortle from the alley. "Hoo-heeee."

☰15

Clinton on Patrol

Behind the closed door of the Knockwurst house, Burton and Little Brother stood, unmoving, enchanted. They had stepped into the gentle sounds of springtime. Even Clinton was still, listening.

The air was a-lilt with soft music. Delicate trills and skipping twitters wove and twined around themselves in perfect time and lovely harmony. Edisonia had come home from Kirksville, that was clear. And the harp-flute had reached the heights of perfection.

But when had she come home? And Papa? Burton and Little Brother had been too wrapped up in the invention to notice.

The music drew them. In wonder and delight, they tiptoed through the kitchen, which was tangy with the scent of good things baking in the oven. Through the dining room, where the table was already set for dinner. And into the living room.

Mama looked up at them and lifted a finger to her lips. Be still! Don't disturb Sister! Smiling proudly, she turned her attention back to Edisonia.

Papa was in his rocking chair, his hands folded across his round middle, listening with a proud smile. He rocked in time to the music.

Clinton trotted directly to Edisonia and curled up at the foot of the harp. Clinton adored music. Especially when it warbled and chirped and tweeted as was now happening.

Still clutching the invention, Burton hunkered down on the floor in the bay windows. Little Brother joined him. And for a while, bathed in beautiful music, they forgot all about the amazing invention.

A radiant smile on her face, her eyes closed with the loveliness of it all, Edisonia ran her fingers up the harp strings. Sound rippled through the room. With almost no effort on her part, the flute whispered its woodsy music. Staccato, legato, sforzando,

111

diminuendo—the two instruments played "Home on the Range" as it had never been played before.

At last, with a final run up and down the strings, Edisonia breathed a pleased sigh. She sat back and turned her twinkliest smile on her family. "There. That's the way it's supposed to sound."

"The music world will be changed forevermore," sighed Mama.

"Music of the spheres, truly so," said Papa.

"What's music of—" Little Brother started to ask. Nobody heard him.

"What did you do?" asked Burton. "I mean, how did you work out the problem?"

Little Brother got up and went to the encyclopedia.

"I watched the musicians in Kirksville," Edisonia said happily. "They're world-class, you know. I especially watched the harpist. All week, I watched him. Last night, during the second movement of Papa's concerto—"

"You forgot to turn the page, Sister," said Papa.

"I was so excited," said Edisonia.

"Things like that happen when you get excited," said Burton.

"It didn't matter," said Papa. "I knew that part by heart."

"Just like that"—Edisonia snapped her fingers—

"I knew I needed another pedal on the harp."

"And she did it," said Mama. "She didn't even take her bag to her room when she got home. She just took out her spare parts kit and she added the pedal while I made dinner."

Dinner was a very special event that evening.

Because Papa and Edisonia had returned from Papa's concert with the Kirksville Philharmonic Orchestra. "A most singular musical evening," the music critic of the *Tri-County Record* had said.

Because Edisonia had put the finishing touches on her harp-flute.

Because Burton had finished his invention.

Papa placed the skateboard on the table for a centerpiece where all could admire it while they ate. Mama put a pot of ivy and some candles on it.

"Music of the spheres," said Little Brother, coming to the table late. "A man called Pythagoras—" He chewed up that long, hard name.

"I think you mean Pih-THAG-or-us," Mama corrected him. "He was a truly great Greek mathematician."

"He said that everything in Nature is in harmony and that the planets make music and that—"

The telephone rang.

"I'll get it," said Edisonia, slipping out of her chair and skipping into the hall. "Hello?" she said into the phone. "Hello? Hello?"

"That's funny," she said, coming back to the table. "Nobody was there. I thought somebody said who. Only when I said 'Who who?' they didn't answer."

"Well, if somebody who isn't there is going to call us," said Mama, "I do wish they wouldn't call at dinnertime."

"You are absolutely right, my love," said Papa. "Dinnertime is family time, and nobody should interrupt us . . . er . . . not interrupt us while—"

"Planets are spheres," said Little Brother. "That means round things. There's all kinds of beautiful music in outer space."

"I'd like to hear it," said Edisonia. "Papa, can we go there on vacation sometime?"

They went on with dinner, a new dish that Mama had invented that very day. Made of rutabagas and garbanzo beans, it was a ruta-banzo pie. Their dessert was raspberry-orange-chocolate-peanut-butter parfait in puff pastry.

114

Nobody heard the sounds of someone tiptoeing around outside the house breathing little hoo-hee sighs. Nobody but Clinton. He padded to the front door and growled. He padded to the back door and growled. He never got around to eating dinner, so busy was he keeping track of all that tiptoeing.

Burton went to bed that night thinking about the end of spring break and the first day of school tomorrow. He had accomplished something during the break, all right. He smiled. The invention was under his bed. He leaned down to look at it. It looked great, even seen upside down. He smiled again and turned off the light.

Clinton patrolled the house all that night.

Outside, someone tiptoed around the yard, stopping at every door and window. But Clinton was always there, on the inside.

"Drat," came a voice from the darkness. "Drat that dog. He's too smart for his own good."

"Ahhh-ooooooo," Clinton howled—but softly, softly, so as not to awaken his family. He seemed to agree.

≡16

Watch Out, Burton!

The invention rested under Burton's bed, safely out of sight. It was protected by the automatic bed-maker. Burton had made a few changes in the bed-maker that morning—after it tidied up the rumpled covers, of course. He had added a siren and a snatch-and-hold arm. If anyone touched the invention, the siren would start screeching and the snatch-and-hold arm would grab the toucher and hang on until somebody released it.

Little Brother held up the extra-big super-tough

padlock that had been on the workshop door. "I'll put this on your bedroom door," he said.

"Maybe Clinton can guard the yard until I come for the invention this afternoon," said Burton. "Will you do that, boy? Hm?" He gave Clinton a good, rough patting.

Clinton rolled over and wriggled and sat up. His eyes said that guarding the yard on this particular day was the only thing in life he wanted to do.

"We'll have to tie him," said Little Brother. "But let's use a rope that's long enough to give him the run of the place, front and back. Nobody will get past Clinton. Right, boy?"

"Ah-ooooo," said Clinton.

Little Brother followed Burton outside. "Burt?" he said, "you'll wait for me this afternoon, won't you? I mean, you won't start the demo before I get there, will you?"

Start the demonstration without Little Brother? After all his looking up and delivery of information? Not to mention his good, sensible questions. Burton promised. Little Brother had a big investment of himself in the invention. Burton would see that he wasn't left out of the fun part of things.

Tish and Jonathan and Kevin—with his lariat looped over his shoulder—were waiting out front for Burton. They eyed him closely when he came down the drive. He wasn't carrying anything. He didn't have a big lumpy something strapped to his back. So . . . he wasn't bringing the invention to school. They let out a chorus of disappointed sighs.

"Hey, you said we'd see the invention today," Kevin reminded him.

"After school," said Burton. "Like I said. In the school yard. I'm going to do a demonstration."

The leaves on the horse chestnut tree in the yard next door quivered. "Ha-hoooo," came a soft, pleased sound from the treetop. The invention was still inside the house, then. With the boy away all day, perhaps . . . The ha-hooo changed to a discouraged hoo-ha when Clinton came bounding around the side of the house.

There would be no getting near the Knockwurst house today.

Well, then. After school, then. When the boy came to get his whatever-it-was . . . Or later, in the school yard. But time was running out. Today. He had to get hold of that invention today.

A day with Miss Doyle was never easy to get through. But this one was uncommonly hard. Being as how it was the first day after spring break. And being as how Burton was looking forward to the afternoon and the demo.

Miss Doyle chose this day to come down on them about their spelling.

Rhythm is a tricky word, even for musicians. Burton didn't get it right. But neither did Tish, and she was the best speller in the room.

And then there was *frolic*. Burton spelled it with a *K*. Why did Miss Doyle have to use so many big words? Burton wasn't quite sure what *frolic* meant. It sounded like a sickness a baby might get.

Altogether, then, it was a wordy—not to say roaring—day.

Burton was the first one out of the classroom when the bell rang. He dashed home. He dashed through the kitchen, right past the refrigerator, without looking to see what was in there waiting to be munched on. He dashed up the stairs and into his bedroom and turned off the automatic-bed-maker–invention-watcher. He wriggled under the bed, wriggled back out with the invention, and dashed downstairs. Then he remembered something, dashed back upstairs, grabbed a pink plastic bag from his dresser, and headed outside. He was off like a shot.

This was it!

No further need to keep the board covered.

Forget about walking—that would be too slow.

He rolled down the driveway and out onto the sidewalk, heading back to school. He didn't extend the wings and rockets. Those had to wait for the wide open spaces of the school yard. But even without them, he was the hottest kid on Petunia Street.

He didn't notice a knobby-kneed girl with braids peeking out from behind a fence across the street.

Where—hoo-hee—were the boy's rockets? Odd. Didn't the invention have something to do with rockets? With flight? Most peculiar. Could it be that the boy's skateboard was the invention? Oh, that couldn't be!

The girl took off at a sprint, her braids bouncing as she ran, the scarlet poppies covering her ears fluttering and flapping.

Careful to look both ways, Burton crossed Zinnia Street and Aspidistra Drive. Passing the supermarket on Tulip Street, he didn't notice Merrill Frobusher doing a rail slide in the parking lot.

Merrill noticed Burton, though. His eyes narrowed. He pushed off and rode his board after him.

Tish and Jonathan and Kevin were waiting out in front of school. They watched Burton approach down the street.

"Hey, the invention is a skateboard."

"Wow! Look at him move!"

"Whadaya know—here comes Frobusher."

"Hey, who's that funny-looking girl?"

Burton whipped to a stop in front of the kids and dismounted.

Merrill skidded to a halt beside him and did the Frobusher specialty, flipping his board up into his arms.

120

The "girl" was close behind Merrill, coming on at a sprint. Her eyes glittered when she saw the skateboard at Burton's feet, unguarded, just standing there, practically asking to be picked up. Excited, she couldn't keep a hop-skip out of her churning legs.

Click! For Jonathan, everything fell into place. Skipping—that was it. The funny little guy who had followed Burton in the park skipped. So had that weird old lady. And the delivery man.

"It's him!" yelled Jonathan, pointing. "It's the spy guy in disguise."

The "girl" dove for the invention. Now! Get it now and make a fast getaway.

"Oh, no you don't!" yelled Kevin, tossing his lariat. It looped down over the girl. But clutching the skateboard to her chest, she continued to run, pulling Kevin after her.

Tish was fast on her feet, too. "You mustn't take Burt's invention," she yelled in a ladylike voice. Dancing forward on her toes, she placed a neat karate chop somewhere south of the girl's braids.

"Ooooooooof!" The girl sank to the ground.

Off flew the wig. Away fluttered the poppies. Out popped a pair of distinguished ears that continued to quiver even as Professor Savvy sprawled on the ground.

Jonathan leaned down and lifted the skateboard out of his arms. "Sorry, bub," he said, "but we aren't gonna let you get away with Burt's invention."

Kevin pulled his rope tight, winding it around the professor's ankles. "Sorry, pardner," he drawled. "We don't like it when you bad guys try to rob a good guy."

"Whoever you are," said Tish, leaning down, "you ought to know that your skirts are way up above your knees. That isn't ladylike, you know." She smiled sweetly.

Little Brother came running into the school yard, practically towed by Clinton on his leash. "I didn't miss it, did I?" he called. "We aren't late for the demo, are we?"

122

He and Clinton saw the professor at the exact same moment. Clinton made a dive for him.

"Don't bite, Clinton! Don't bite!" yelled Little Brother, barely managing to hang onto Clinton. Then he took in the professor's dress and the wig and flowers scattered around him. "But," he added, "I think you'd better keep an eye on him, Clint."

Clinton looked as though—if he could have—he would have smiled as he stood guard over Professor Savvy. He didn't bite. But the professor didn't move, either.

≡17

Who's a Coward!

And that's how the professor saw everything that happened after that— lying flat on his back, with four dratted kids and a dratted dog standing guard over him.

"Listen, Knockwurst," sneered Merrill Frobusher, "I saw you in the park the other day. Think you're pretty smart, don't you?"

"I don't think I'm so smart," Burton said evenly. He didn't want to tangle with Frobusher today.

"Well, let me tell you," said Merrill. "You may be good on your board. But you're not as good as I am, and I'm going to prove it. Right now. I challenge you to a contest."

"Aw, come on, Frobusher," said Burton, who only wanted to get on with his demonstration. "You don't want to do that."

"Whatsa matter," taunted Merrill. "You some kind of coward?"

That stung! Burton knew he wasn't a coward. He just was not interested in a duel with Frobusher. And anyway, even though Frobusher didn't know it, Burton was doing him a favor—he was trying to be fair. For no matter what Frobusher did on his skateboard, he would certainly be outclassed by Burton riding on the invention. "Look," he said, "this really isn't a regular skateboard."

"Ha!" sneered Merrill. "If something looks like a duck and quacks like a duck, it *is* a duck. Well, that looks like a skateboard and it acts like a skateboard—so it *is* a skateboard. You want to meet my challenge? Or are you too scared?"

"Okay," sighed Burton. He couldn't get out of this. "But don't say I didn't warn you."

"I'll call the shots," said Merrill. "See if you can do what I do. Match my style."

He mounted his skateboard, built up speed, and thundered toward a series of jagged cracks in the cement. There were three of them, close together, and they were bad. Any one of them could send a skater into a nosedive.

Riding with ease, half turned, his knees bent, Merrill ollied over them. The first . . . the second . . . the third. He was in control and the ollies were perfect, every one.

A ledge ran the length of the school beneath the first floor windows. He leaned down, one hand on the deck, leaped up onto the ledge, and landed smoothly, without a wobble. He rode the narrow ledge for its entire length and sailed off, landing on the board, easily, gracefully. A long nose slide brought him to a standstill in front of Burton.

It had been quite a display. The kids let out their breaths. You had to admire skill like that. It was an art.

"Like I said, match my style." Merrill grinned maddeningly. "Which you can't," he added.

"You're forcing me into this, Frobusher," said Burton.

Merrill smirked at him. "You talk a good game, Knockwurst."

Burton handed the pink plastic bag to Tish for safekeeping and took the invention from Jonathan. "Just remember—I warned you, Frobusher."

"Good luck, Burt," Tish said softly.

"He doesn't need luck," said Little Brother. "He's

126

got the Va-ROOOM Machine. You'll see."

Va-ROOOM Machine! Little Brother had named the invention.

Burton started from well back to give himself room to build speed. The wheels, those wonderful wheels, moved smoothly, with a sound of silken softness. He headed for the sawtooth cracks. Awkwardly placed, they looked like the Rocky Mountains in miniature. Could he? Without using the rockets? He had to! Using the rockets for this part of the demo wouldn't be fair competition.

He did it. He ollied over them. One. Two. Three.

"Ya-hoooo," yodeled Kevin.

Coming up was the ledge under the windows. It was high, higher than anything he had ever attempted. But he had to do this one under his own power, too. He crouched, balanced with one hand on the board, and—zippo—he landed on the narrow strip of concrete. He rode the entire length, his arms in the air.

Okay. Enough of this ordinary stuff. This was more than a contest with Merrill Frobusher. It was, after all, a demonstration of what the invention could do.

He fingered the remote. The wings moved into position. With a soft sputter—the contented hippopotamus sound—the rockets kicked in.

127

The invention lifted off the ledge and continued upward. With a swishing hiss, it carried him past the astonished faces of Merrill and the others at nose level.

Merrill's jaw went slack. His mouth dropped open.

The professor watched with a sickly smile. So. The boy's invention did have to do with rockets, with flight. Ha-hoooo.

"Let 'er rip, Burt," shouted Little Brother.

Kevin hopped up and down. "Rev it up, Burt."

Once, twice, three times, Burt circled the school yard. On the fourth go-around, he sailed past Miss Doyle looking out the classroom window. How long had she been there watching? "Burton Bell Whitney Knockwurst," she roared. Nothing followed. Miss Doyle was speechless.

This was fun! This was better than a roller coaster ride! Burton felt like a bird.

Okay. Time now for the last part of the demo. He tapped the remote again and felt his shoes tighten onto the deck. Ready? Go for it!

He did a loop-the-loop and followed it from high up with a dive. He deliberately stalled when he almost reached the ground, brought the nose of the board back up, and circled the school yard a last time.

128

The invention was great! It did everything he had known it would and could probably do even better things. But he needed practice before he tried any more tricks.

He turned off the shoe grips, shut down the rockets, and slid to a landing.

Merrill, in the sudden silence, closed his mouth and gulped. "I never saw anything like that," he said. He looked as though he was about to cry.

"Hey, it's okay, Frobusher," said Burton. "I told you this isn't a regular skateboard. And," he added generously, "I have to admit I really can't match your personal riding style."

"Wow!" breathed Kevin. "That's what I call speed. Can I ride it, Burt? Can I give it a try? Can I, huh?"

"You!"

Miss Doyle's voice boomed over the school yard. They all turned to the windows.

"You there!" roared Miss Doyle. "Theophilus"— she pronounced it Thee-OPH-ih-lus—"Savarino. I recognize you in spite of that ridiculous dress you have on. Come in to see me at once. Do you hear? Now, I say."

"Yes, ma'am," said Professor Savvy. He was pale—and not from the bump on his head he had taken when Tish decked him. "I'm coming," he

129

called. "If," he added in an undertone to Kevin, "you will be so kind as to remove your rope from my ankles. And," he added as Clinton growled, "if somebody will call off this . . . this . . . canine monster."

≡ 18

Cloudhoppers

*M*iss Doyle sat at her desk, her shoes off, resting her toes. Every inch of the chalkboard behind her was filled with writing.

> *I will never, never take anyone's*
> *invention ever again.*
> *I will never, never take anyone's*
> *invention ever again.*

Professor Savvy was starting in on the chalkboard on the east wall. He had to stand on tiptoes to reach the top of the board.

Miss Doyle fixed him with her gimlet eye. "I," she roared at his back, "am ashamed that a former pupil of mine is not only a failed inventor—how *could* you, Theophilus!—but one who acts in such an underhanded, shameful, unscrupulous, dishonest manner."

Miss Doyle knew all about Professor Savvy. Leaning out the window, waiting for him to come indoors, she had questioned Jonathan and Kevin and Tish.

"I'm sorry, ma'am," muttered the professor.

"Speak up," roared Miss Doyle. "Didn't I teach you to speak loud and clear?"

"I'm sorry, ma'am," said the professor, loud and clear. "Hoo-hee, he added under his breath, "I'll say I'm sorry!"

"Didn't I teach you that the only way to success is good, hard work?" continued Miss Doyle.

"Yes, ma'am."

"And didn't I tell you often that you had promise, but that you would have to work to make it flower into something special?"

"Yes, ma'am." The professor scribbled at breakneck speed, to finish his punishment as quickly as possible.

Wham! Miss Doyle's hand came down on her desk with a slap that sounded like an explosion.

The professor jumped.

132

"I will not—do you hear?—I will not put up with sloppy handwriting. Your *T*s, Theophilus. Your *L*s. Make them tall and graceful."

The professor's shoulders slumped in misery. "Yes, ma'am," he said without a hoo or a hee or a ha.

There was a sound at the door. Miss Doyle looked up.

Burton came into the classroom. He was swinging the pink plastic bag by its pink string. "I've brought you something, Miss Doyle," he said.

Miss Doyle watched him approach her desk. "Well, Burton Bell Whitney Knockwurst," she said in a friendly half roar, "you certainly did put on a display of considerable virtuosity—that is to say skill—this afternoon."

"Thank you, ma'am," said Burton. The warm afterglow of the successful demonstration was still with him.

"But I am not sure," Miss Doyle continued, "whether I applaud your performance or the contraption you were riding."

At that moment there was a triumphant cry from the school yard. It sounded almost like a cowboy riding a bucking bronco. They turned just in time to see Kevin arc upward, pass the window, and descend groundward. "Ya-hoooo," he yelled. "Ya-hooooo!" He was riding the skateboard.

Miss Doyle turned pale. "Burton Bell Whitney Knockwurst, I wonder if you quite know what you have unleashed on the world."

Burton got the picture. He saw what she meant. He had to admit he had not thought about the invention in the way she meant.

"You," roared Miss Doyle, "are going to have to invent a whole set of rules to govern what children must and must not do on your invention."

"Yes, ma'am," said Burton. But he didn't want to think about that now. He had something for Miss Doyle. He laid the pink plastic bag on her desk. "I invented something for you, ma'am."

Miss Doyle reached into the bag and pulled out a pair of shoes. She looked at Burton, a question on her face.

"They're cloudhoppers, ma'am," Burton explained.

Miss Doyle still did not understand.

"Well, see," said Burton, "you'll walk on air in these cloudhoppers. You'll never have hurting toes again."

Miss Doyle turned pink. "Why, my dear boy," she said. Her voice was almost tender. Tender! It was a very peculiar voice, coming from Tilly Doyle.

"Try them on," said Burton. "I'm pretty sure they will fit."

"Ha-hooo," came an excited sound from the chalkboard. "Great idea you've got there, lad. Great—"

"Theophilus Savarino," roared Miss Doyle, "tend to your punishment."

"Yes, ma'am," the professor said meekly. He turned back to his writing, and Miss Doyle slid her feet into the cloudhoppers and tied the laces. She stood up.

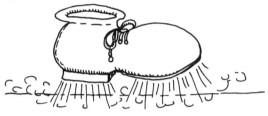

A gentle sigh came from the shoes. They lifted slightly off the floor.

Miss Doyle walked from her desk to the window. On air.

She walked the length of the room. On air.

"What?" she stuttered, turning to Burton. Miss Doyle never stuttered. "How?" she murmured. Miss Doyle never murmured.

Burton began to feel uncomfortable. He didn't quite know what to say to a stuttering, murmuring Miss Doyle. "Uh," he said, "uh, I thought about them when I was working on the invention. They're like Hovercraft, those aircraft that ride on a cushion of air."

"I am," said Miss Doyle, "quite overcome." Her

135

eyes glistened. Were those tears in her eyes? Tears of happiness?

Burton squirmed. He had spent a long time getting used to a roaring Tilly Doyle. A boy could deal with a roaring Miss Doyle. But a softhearted Miss Doyle? Burton didn't know how to act.

"I feel," Miss Doyle said softly, dabbing at her eyes, "positively"—she started to smile—"absolutely"—her smile broadened—"like a good frolic," she said. She laughed out loud and showed what that hard word meant. She frolicked around the room. She skipped up and down the aisles. She twirled on her toes. She was as frisky as a lamb in springtime.

Another wild cry came from the school yard. "Yippeeeee!"

Kevin flew past the windows, upside down. He righted himself just before he disappeared from view.

Miss Doyle stopped in mid-frolic. "Harumph," she said. It was practically a normal Tilly Doyle harumph. "I think," she said, walking sedately to her desk, "that you, Burton Bell Whitney Knockwurst"—her voice grew louder with every word—"had better settle down right this very minute and invent those rules." *Rules* came out sounding like a roar. "I think," she boomed, "that you

136

will not leave this room until you complete those rules."

Burton felt better. He let out a relieved sigh. A roaring Tilly Doyle was someone a boy knew how to handle. He went to his desk and got out his notebook.

Miss Doyle sank into her chair. She did not kick off the cloudhoppers.

The classroom was quiet except for the screeek of chalk on the board.

Miss Doyle wriggled her toes inside the cloudhoppers and looked at peace with the world.

Theophilus Savarino—the professor—scratched away at the chalkboard, careful to make his *T*s and *L*s tall and graceful.

Burton wrote the first line of his rules for use of the Va-ROOOM Machine:

Rule 1. Do not use the Va-ROOOM Machine when any grown-ups are around. It scares them. Rule 2. Be sure to turn on the shoe grips before . . . you . . .

He looked out the window. The leaves were starting to come out on the trees. They made a lacy tracery against the cloud-blown spring sky. In that lacy pattern he saw the shape of a . . . was that a frog? . . . of a flower? . . . maybe . . . of . . . of . . . He forgot about the rules he was supposed to be writing.

That shape! Up there at the top of the tallest tree. Was that . . . no, it couldn't be. . . . Eureka! It was. It was a time machine.

A time machine could take a person back to the day when that tree was just a little bitty willow sapling! But if the tree was a sapling, would the person in the time machine turn back into a baby? Well, maybe if . . . an . . . inventor . . .

Burton smiled and dreamed on. He was onto something big. He was sure of it.